SPANISH INQUISITION

Recent Titles by Elizabeth Darrell from Severn House

BEYOND ALL FRONTIERS
SCARLET SHADOWS
FORGET THE GLORY
THE RICE DRAGON
SHADOWS OVER THE SUN

UNSUNG HEROES
FLIGHT TO ANYWHERE

The Max Rydal Mysteries

RUSSIAN ROULETTE
CHINESE PUZZLE
CZECH MATE
DUTCH COURAGE
FRENCH LEAVE
INDIAN SUMMER
SCOTCH MIST

SPANISH INQUISITION

Elizabeth Darrell

This first world edition published 2012
in Great Britain and in the USA by
SEVERN HOUSE PUBLISHERS LTD of
9–15 High Street, Sutton, Surrey, England, SM1 1DF.

British Library Cataloguing in Publication Data

Darrell, Elizabeth.
  Spanish Inquisition.
  1. Rydal, Max (Fictitious character)–Fiction.
  2. Detective and mystery stories.
  I. Title
  823.9'14-dc23

ISBN-13: 978-0-7278-8186-1 (cased)

All Severn House titles are printed on acid-free paper.

Severn House Publishers support The Forest Stewardship Council [FSC],
the leading international forest certification organisation. All our titles that
are printed on Greenpeace-approved FSC-certified paper carry the FSC logo.

FSC
www.fsc.org

MIX
Paper from
responsible sources
FSC® C018575

Typeset by Palimpsest Book Production Ltd.,
Falkirk, Stirlingshire, Scotland.
Printed and bound in Great Britain by
MPG Books Ltd., Bodmin, Cornwall.

ACKNOWLEDGEMENTS

My thanks to all the servicemen and women who have given me their willing help with the Max Rydal series over the years which gave me the opportunity to learn so much about the complex and valuable work they do. Particular thanks this time to Captain Jason Budding of the Royal Signals Training Development Team, Blandford Camp.

ONE

The party was still going strong at midnight, long after the VIP guests had departed. Cynically eyeing those around him Sergeant Major Tom Black thought it was more a mutual admiration gathering than a party. The final performance of *Carmen* staged by the Operatic Society had ended two hours ago, yet members of the cast and backstage crew were still hugging, kissing, wiping away tears as they lapped up praise heaped upon them by friends and family.

Tom had no artistic leanings. He had only attended the performance, and remained for this artificial shenanigan, because his wife had been happily and enthusiastically engaged during her sixth and seventh months of pregnancy in making costumes for 'assorted villagers' who comprised most of the chorus. She deserved her share of the congratulations tonight.

Outnumbered four to one by Nora, and their daughters who were agog to mingle with the sexily-clad matadors and picadors, Tom had to make the best of this wasted Saturday evening by downing a couple of beers in a quiet corner, and eating heartily of the refreshments laid on by willing volunteers. From his refuge he kept his eye on one of the picadors, reluctantly conceding that he looked good in tight breeches and a highly ornate coat.

On learning of Phil Piercey's desire to perform in *Carmen* Tom had told his sergeant to forget it, saying, 'You're a detective in the army's police force, for God's sake, not a poncy chorus boy who abandons pursuit of criminal cases two evenings a week to go off and pretend he's a bloody bullfighter who *sings*!'

However, after thinking it over, Tom had withdrawn his objection. Piercey was a maverick, a sharp investigator who defied rules to follow obscure leads that might put him ahead of the rest of the team. Getting involved with this production would give him less time to go out on a limb, and maybe keep him out of Tom's hair during this present command of 26 Section, Special Investigation Branch while Captain Max Rydal recovered from injuries sustained during an explosion six weeks before Christmas.

For four months Tom had been running 26 Section, a duty he was perfectly capable of handling. What made it uneasy was the predilection of the Regional Commander to arrive without warning and interfere in cases that were going perfectly well. Tom could do nothing about Major Keith Pinkney's well-intentioned supervision, but to have Phil Piercey subdued by unrequited lust would compensate in some degree.

It was general knowledge that it was not for the pleasure of singing that the womanizing sergeant was strutting his stuff in the theatre on the military base, earning taunts from his colleagues and sniggers from squaddies who had fallen foul of him in the past.

Corporal Maria Norton, playing the title role, had long black hair, fiery black eyes, a generously rounded figure and the allure of a young woman whose mother was Castillian. Piercey had fallen heavily for her sultry charm and was in hot, but apparently fruitless, pursuit. Redcaps, if not actually hated by the average soldier, were certainly given a wide berth whenever possible, but the Operatic Society had accepted Piercey because the opera required a strong male chorus and he had an unexpectedly good baritone voice to go with a fine muscular body.

Rumour had it that Maria Norton was playing with Piercey the way Carmen plays with her hapless military guard, which news pleased the members of 26 Section, who all agreed it was time the boot was on the other foot. From his corner at the party Tom watched with amusement as Piercey competed with several other hopefuls to hold Maria's attention for longer than half a minute, and saw that rumour had it right. The voluptuous corporal knew exactly how to excite then deflate, and Piercey was getting the full treatment.

Tom's pleasure in this soon ended when he spotted his eldest daughter Maggie, fourteen and looking older, being chatted up by a fresh-faced lad in satin breeches that revealed how well endowed he was.

Where the hell was Nora? He started forward, tardily realizing that *he* should have been with his family. The habit of believing the girls were her responsibility, as they so often were, was hard to break. Girls needed their mother once they reached a certain age, but he knew parenting was a dual responsibility and he had been opting out on a night when his wife was entitled to be free to enjoy these end-of-the-run high jinks.

Gathering his protesting children together, he made signals to Nora who was happy to leave, and they went out for the drive back to their rented house halfway between the base and the local town. It was cold, with a full moon and a multitude of stars. The quietness after the noise of the party was welcome to Tom, who wanted to reach home and climb straight into bed. He had had a hectic week and looked forward to a good sleep, with a lie-in in the morning before enjoying a lazy Sunday with his family.

While the female members gossiped about the guests, Tom drove to the main gate lost in thoughts of future Sundays, when he and his son would do man things together. On the day the scan had shown that Nora was carrying a male child this time his delight had been so great he had been struck dumb. He said little on the subject even now, but his mind was storing images of himself and Christopher Black indulging in pastimes fathers and daughters rarely shared.

Reaching the house, they were met by joyous yapping from the puppy which had taken up residence in time for Christmas. There was the usual plea from Beth, the youngest, to take the little dog up to bed, and the usual firm NO! from Tom and Nora in unison. By the time Strudel (a ridiculous name in Tom's view) had been fussed over, given a biscuit and put in the rear garden to reduce the risk of puddles on the storeroom floor in the morning, it was just after one a.m. Half an hour later Tom turned off the bedside light and settled gratefully for sleep, close against Nora's back, having said all he should about the stage costumes she had made. The house fell silent as Tom drifted into slumber wondering about buying a boat to take on the river where Max sculled on Sunday mornings. He could show Christopher how to steer it and then how to operate the outboard motor.

A persistent ringing brought him from his nautical dreams, and he automatically stretched out his hand to the telephone beside him.

'Yes,' he mumbled sleepily.

'Sorry to disturb you, sir, but I think you should come in on this,' said a voice Tom recognized as that of Corporal Babs Turvey, a member of the uniformed police squad on the base.

'Go on,' he said, rolling away from Nora and speaking quietly into the receiver as he noted that it was now three a.m.

'An hour ago Corporal Maria Norton, 5 Signals, staggered in here in a very distressed state. Her face and arms were bruised, her dress was torn and she was generally very dishevelled. I couldn't get much sense from her before she collapsed. I called an ambulance and went with her to the Medical Centre, where they gave her something to make her relax.'

'What has this to do with me?' hissed Tom impatiently.

'Norton claimed she was attacked and assaulted outside the Recreation Centre where there'd been a party after the closing performance of *Carmen*.'

'Rape?'

'She didn't claim full sexual assault, sir, but I've called in Captain Goodey to examine her. The victim is too traumatized to be fully coherent, but she has named her attacker as Phil Piercey. We've got him here.'

'On way,' Tom said in leaden tones.

While driving back to the base Tom's thoughts were muddled, in the extreme. Even though the girl was not crying rape, she had evidently been viciously attacked. Piercey was facing a serious charge which, when fully investigated, could bring the end of his career. Admittedly, Norton had been very obviously playing him like a fish on a hook at the party, and there was no doubting the young sergeant's obsession with her, yet Tom was uncomfortable with the scenario.

Piercey was extrovert, highly experienced and packed with assurance where women were concerned, but he was not a man given to excessive behaviour. Before joining SIB his four years in uniform had been exemplary. Redcaps on patrol had to deal with soldiers who were drunk, abusive, violent – sometimes in large groups – and had to retain their nerve. They were armed for their own protection and anyone liable to lose control and start firing at random would never make the grade and wear the famous red-covered cap.

Tom had been watching Piercey at the party. He had not been deeply under the influence so, unless he had imbibed non-stop after the Black family had departed, it seemed unlikely that alcohol had driven him to assault the provocative corporal. Torn between the wish to protect one of his own team, and the victim's positive identification, Tom had to consider the possibility that Piercey had reacted thus because he had never before been rejected by a woman he wanted, and publicly so. All in all, Tom felt unhappy as he turned in through the main gate, acknowledging the wave of recognition from the night guard who raised the barrier for him.

Babs Turvey looked grave when he entered the police post. Although Piercey was SIB he was also a member of the Corps, and therefore also a subject of regimental concern for her and Corporal Meacher, who was retrieving any calls that came in during the night hours.

'Anything yet from the MO?' he asked sharply.

Babs shook her head.

'Has Phil offered any defence?'

'No. When Jeff and I woke him and told him he was under arrest on suspicion, he looked gobsmacked. Hasn't said a word apart from asking for you to be contacted.'

Tom nodded. 'Have you taken a DNA swab?'

'No, sir. As SIB will be taking over as of now we've left that to you. We have the clothes he was wearing.' She indicated a bag in the corner of the small outer office. 'His underwear hasn't been washed, and he had apparently returned to his room still in his stage costume. The victim was also wearing hers when she was attacked. And a vast amount of theatrical make-up.'

Tom gave a heavy sigh. 'And she's definite about her attacker's identity?'

'Named him several times.' Babs wagged her head in a faintly resigned gesture. 'Why would she dob Phil in if he didn't do it?'

'Can you rustle up some tea and bring it to the interview room?' asked Tom, declining to answer that. Until he had heard Piercey's version of what had happened he was not prepared to form any conclusions.

Even so, when Tom walked in to the cell-like room containing just a bare table and four chairs he came close to doing just that. The man he knew as supremely assured and well able to handle anything had very obviously been knocked for six. In a dark green track suit, brown hair mussed from sleep, the Cornish sergeant was hunched over the table with his head in his hands. When he glanced up the light brown eyes so often alive with fervour were blank with shock. Experience told Tom this was surely an innocent man.

'Why's she doing this to me?' Piercey asked huskily. 'Why?'

'Because you attacked her?' suggested Tom.

'You'll find no evidence of that.' Piercey shook his head. 'She's lying. Why would a woman protect a man who had beaten her up?'

Tom sat facing him across the table. 'You've been in this game long enough to know people do inexplicable things.'

'Was she raped?'

'Captain Goodey's examining her now. Babs Turvey says the girl showed signs of severe physical assault, but we won't have the full picture until we receive the Doc's assessment.'

Babs entered with two mugs of tea and left without a word. Then Tom told Piercey to remove the top of his track suit and place his hands flat on the table. If the man resented this order he showed no sign of it. The shadow of shock still dulled his expression as he pulled off the green garment and slapped his palms down on the metal table top. There was no sign of scratching or bruising on Piercey's body and knuckles to suggest resistance to an attack by him. There would have to be a full medical examination, but Tom was pleased by this lack of evidence, and proceeded.

'OK, tell me what happened between you and Maria Norton.'

'*Nothing* happened.'

'Why didn't you change out of costume before you went to your quarters? Surely it's usual practice to leave all theatrical gear on the premises.'

'I'd have taken it there in the morning. *This* morning.'

'That didn't answer my question.'

'I left in a hurry.'

'Why?'

'Bill Jensen was waiting to lock up.'

'So most people had already departed?'

'Most, yes.'

'Not Maria Norton?'

'No.'

'So you were there alone with her?'

'Not really.'

'Yes or no,' snapped Tom.

'We were the only ones backstage. Bill Jensen was out front with . . .' He frowned trying to remember. 'I think two of the chorus girls were chatting with some of the lads, making plans for Sunday. *Today,*' he added heavily.

'Names?'

'Christ, I don't know, I only heard their voices.'

'Go on.'

It took a moment or two for Piercey to work up to confessing something so personal. 'I've never experienced with another woman what I felt for her. She laughed it off; said she'd heard all about my reputation. Nothing I said made her take me seriously. She'd lead me on, then do the same with Frank Mellor, Andy Sloman or Evan Davies. Right in front of me.'

Knowing Piercey was revealing with every word that he had a strong motive for taking revenge for the humiliations, Tom nevertheless continued with his probing. 'She flirted with a number of men in the cast?'

'I thought it was her way of coping with all the guys who tried it on with her.'

'One of whom was you. Go on!'

The other man took a long breath and exhaled slowly. 'I had to convince her that I meant what I said.'

'How convince her?'

The stricken sergeant's expression said it all.

'You kissed and fondled her? Took advantage of your isolation backstage to get what she'd promised then snatched away?'

'It wasn't like that. Everyone had been hugging and congratulating her throughout the evening. I just wanted to do the same; show her how terrific she had been in the show.'

Tom slapped his palm on the table in anger. 'Balls! After saying how you felt about her, d'you take me for an idiot? You saw your chance and went in strong to show you're not a man to be messed with. You were determined to have what she'd dangled in front of you then withdrawn, humiliating you in front of other guys who wanted a bit of nookie, too.'

'No!'

'Yes! No jury would believe that a man whose passion has been publicly ridiculed by a woman, then embraced her merely to congratulate her on her singing and acting. Pull yourself together, man!' Leaving a moment or two to let that sink in, Tom turned the screw further. 'You lost control and embarked on the really rough stuff. How drunk were you?'

Piercey began to fight back as the truth of his situation started to register. 'Not enough to do what she accused me of in an outraged yell designed to be heard by those out front.'

'You're saying she put on an act for the benefit of anyone still in the theatre; that you weren't trying to have it off with her in her dressing room?'

'Christ, what d'you take me for?' demanded Piercey angrily.

'It's a case of her word against yours,' Tom continued, determined to get at the truth. 'So what happened next?'

Visibly roused, Piercey said, 'She ran out to join the others, making out she needed their protection. A couple of guys looked set to have a go at me, so I left through the stage door and returned to my room. I'd had enough of her play acting.'

'Did anyone see you arrive at the Mess? I heard the CCTV is on the blink again.'

'Not unless they were watching from their window. I didn't meet anyone on the way in. I took a shower and sat on my bed with a six-pack. Four cans were empty when Babs and Jeff shook me awake, so if you breathalyse me now my registered alcohol intake will be much higher than when I left the theatre.'

'They'll have sealed your room so the cans will be there, but no way can you prove when you emptied them.'

Tom had known and worked with this man for three years and, apart from their personality clash, he believed Piercey to be genuinely stunned by this charge made against him. It was going to be a hell of a case to handle. Tom had himself seen Piercey almost slavering over Maria Norton at the party, and he had little doubt that the interlude backstage had been far more impassioned than a congratulatory hug. Even so, he well believed Norton's theatrical act which had made other men aggressive in her defence would cause any infatuated male to try to escape further humiliation by slinking away to lick his wounds. Unfortunately, it could also be seen as a last straw situation by jurors, who might well then believe Piercey had lain in wait to take his revenge on her.

During violent assaults the perpetrator left samples of DNA on the victim from hair, skin, clothing, spittle and other sources. If Piercey was innocent the absence of his DNA on Maria Norton would be enough to prove it, Unfortunately, that passionate embrace backstage negated that line of defence. Yes, it was a hell of a case, and Keith Pinkney was certain to descend on 26 Section and take over.

'Why's she doing this to me?'

The sudden repetition brought Tom from his thoughts, and he answered sharply, 'Because you made her hate you enough. It's known as sexual harassment.'

Piercey's eyes narrowed as he asked harshly, 'And what's what I've done to make *you* hate me known as? I've always thought you were a shrewd and unbiased investigator, but you've got me marked guilty as charged. Do you see this as the way to get rid of me at last?'

Tom bit back a lashing reply; gave himself time to smother his anger. 'I'll forget you said that and concentrate on being a shrewd and unbiased investigator. Babs will supply you with pen and paper to write your account of your movements after you heard the two men vow to see to you on Maria's behalf and you slipped out through the stage door, until you returned to your room. After a medical examination and taking of DNA samples from you, you can then bed down in one of the cells in our headquarters until I've managed to interview Corporal Norton and heard the MO's report on her injuries.' He got to his feet. 'The cell door will not be locked. You will simply be helping me with my inquiry.'

After installing Piercey at Headquarters, with a blanket and a pillow, Tom read through the written statement feeling certain the accused sergeant had been economical with the truth concerning that backstage encounter. He would question Piercey again once he had heard from Maria Norton just how aggressive she claimed her frustrated admirer had been.

Crossing to the Medical Centre, Tom entered the dimly lit building and went to Clare Goodey's consulting room hoping she would by now have a full report of the victim's injuries. Two and a half hours had passed since Babs Turvey had brought her there by ambulance.

Dressed in grey trousers and a matching roll neck jumper, the blonde doctor was compiling her notes, head bent to the task. Tom gave a quiet greeting from the doorway, and she glanced up with a nod.

'I guessed you'd be along soon. The attacker was one of yours, I gather.'

'So she claims.'

Clare gazed at him shrewdly. 'Innocent until . . . ?' She indicated the chair before her desk. 'Take a seat and I'll give you the results of my examination.'

'Can I speak to her?' he asked as he sat.

'Not until late morning. She's still in shock and under sedation.' Easing back her chair she thrust a hand through her hair as she flexed her shoulders. 'Her clothes are bagged and tagged ready for forensic examination. She was wearing what looked rather like some kind of stage costume.'

'For the past week she's been singing the title role in *Carmen*. Did you not know?'

She gave a faint smile. 'Not my scene. Opera does little for me. Performed by amateurs even less.'

'She was good, very convincing as a provocative factory girl and, from what I saw at the after-performance party, she wasn't too eager to relinquish the act when the curtain came down.'

'Well, whoever attacked her wasn't acting, Tom. The bruising on her body is the result of a ferocious assault with a bunched fist as well as the back of an open hand. The size and spacing of the bruises indicate a male fist, and the marks around her throat are definitely the result of being seized by a large powerful hand.'

Tom frowned. 'He tried to strangle her?'

'He would surely have succeeded if that had been his aim. I'd say he first grabbed her by the neck and shook her, then began beating her up because she didn't give him the right answers.' She shrugged. 'It's just a guess; you're the expert at getting to the truth.'

By now Tom was more than ever sure Piercey was not responsible. However impassioned he might have been, no way would he have seized the woman by the throat or punched her.

'Has she explained how she came by the bruises?'

'She clammed up; refused to say anything either to me or

to Corporal Wills of the Rape Squad.' Seeing his reaction, she said, 'I called them in. It's usual in cases of extreme violence against a female, you know that.'

'Was she raped?'

'There's no evidence of it. However, she *is* in the early stages of pregnancy.' Clare pursed her lips and gave him a significant look. 'Maybe she broke the news to him. You know how it goes. He's appalled, says it must be aborted. She's defiant, says she wants his baby. He loses it and hits out.'

Getting to his feet, Tom said with a satisfied smile, 'Yes, I know how it goes, and that has to let Piercey off the hook. I know the man. If he was going to be a father he'd be trumpeting the fact all round the base.'

Maria Norton looked a sorry sight lying against piled pillows in the small room used for patients requiring isolation from others who might be in the six-bed ward in the base Medical Centre. The beating seemed also to have subdued her spirit quite drastically, although Tom realized that away from the flamboyance of the stage role this present lacklustre attitude might be her normal mien. He had never encountered this Signals NCO professionally.

After identifying himself, Tom assured her her attacker would be charged and punished just as soon as she outlined to him exactly what had happened outside the Recreation Centre in the early hours of that morning. When she listlessly rolled her head in a negative, he asked if she was indicating that she had no memory of the assault.

Gazing at the blue and white bedcover, she mumbled, 'D'you think I'd forget something like that?'

'So why the shake of the head?'

'I just want to be left alone. Captain Goodey said I need to rest quietly for a few days.'

'Which is what you're doing, Corporal,' he responded briskly. 'I can sit here all day until you feel able to answer my questions, but the sooner I have the truth about who did this to you, and why, the sooner he'll face what he deserves.'

With her gaze seemingly glued to the bedclothes, Norton raised both hands then let them drop in a gesture that irritated Tom with its negativity. What was she playing at?

'You were very eager to tell Corporal Turvey who had knocked you about when you went to the RMP Post for help. You named the person responsible several times, both to her and to Captain Goodey when the ambulance brought you here. Have you had second thoughts on that? Is that the problem?'

'No . . . it was him.'

'Who?'

'Phil Piercey.'

He drew in his breath, 'You're sure of that? It was dark.'

Her expression as she glanced up smacked of derision. 'When someone starts feeling you up, talking dirty, you know bloody well who he is . . . and there was only one of them who didn't understand the meaning of NO!' she added with growing heat. 'He tried it on before we left. I had to fight him off and run out to the auditorium where two of the blokes were all set to sort him out. But he skipped out the rear door, didn't he! Must've waited to get me alone where it was dark.'

'So you didn't leave the building with the men who scared Sergeant Piercey off? Why was that?'

She sought inspiration from the bedcover, eventually coming up with, 'I did, but I realized I'd left something in the dressing room and told them to go ahead and I'd catch up.'

'They didn't offer to go back with you?' At her silence, he asked, 'Had Bill Jensen locked the Centre by then?'

'No,' she returned swiftly. 'He was still there, so the lads didn't need to go with me.'

'I see,' said Tom, knowing all this could be checked with Jensen and the two men. 'Who were this pair of Galahads?'

'Just boys in the chorus. I hardly knew them because I played the lead role, you know.'

'Yes, I watched the performance and attended the party afterwards. You were surrounded by admirers congratulating you even as I and my family left. Why were you still at the Centre with just a few chorus members you barely knew when

Bill Jensen was about to lock up? I find it strange that all the people you had rehearsed and acted with over the space of two months were apparently unconcerned about leaving you in an almost empty theatre at the end of the party.'

'No, not at all. They knew I'd be drained after putting my all into the final performance. The role of Carmen is very demanding. It takes a long time to emerge from it. I was gradually shedding that other personality in the peace and privacy of my dressing room when he came in and began pawing me.'

'He?'

'Phil Piercey.'

'You were still in your stage costume?'

'Which he tried to rip off me.'

'He attempted to strip you? Knowing there were other people nearby?'

Hearing the doubt in Tom's voice, she qualified that comment. 'He said he wanted to.'

'Go on.'

'That's when I ran out to where they were and told them what he'd done.'

'But you just admitted he only said he *wanted* to strip you. He hadn't actually done anything.'

They were suddenly interrupted by an orderly bearing two mugs of tea, along with a plastic cup containing two pills for the patient. Tom wished him further, but Maria Norton took advantage of the break for more histrionics, feigning exhaustion and wincing each time she put the mug to her swollen lips. Fearing the pills were more sedatives, Tom determined to push on while she was drinking the tea.

'So you returned to your dressing room to pick up something you'd left there. What was that?'

'My mobile phone.' It came out pat. Too pat.

'Did Bill Jensen see you?'

She shook her head. 'Don't know.'

'What did you do then?'

'Went out to join the lads who'd offered me a lift.'

'And?'

'The mobile rang. My mother calling to find out how the last night went down. By the time she said goodbye I found the car park was empty. They hadn't waited for me.'

Tom was growing angry with this charade. 'You're saying you stood outside the Recreation Centre wearing no more than a thin dress well after one a.m. and had a long conversation with your mother, knowing people were waiting to take you home?'

She closed her eyes wearily. 'You don't know my mother, sir.'

'So tell me what happened next.'

'That's when he jumped out on me.'

'Where from?' he asked, knowing there were no bushes in the area.

She passed a hand over her brow and sighed. 'He just came out of the darkness and began hitting me, calling me filthy names, saying he'd teach me a lesson.'

'Did he try to strip you, attempt anything sexual?'

'He was just angry and vicious,' she said in a voice growing fainter.

Certain she was about to drift into artificial sedation, Tom asked bluntly, 'Who's the father of your baby, Corporal Norton?'

Her lids shot up and the black eyes that had shown such fire to Don Jose while tormenting him, stared at Tom with hostility. 'I've told you who did this to me. One of yours. Don't pry into my private life, go and sort *him* out! I'm in pain and feel very ill.' With that she began calling for a nurse, and Tom gladly left her to perform another stirring drama.

Max Rydal spotted her from the bedroom window as she turned on to the ochre brick path faded to pale cream by the strong Spanish sun, and he groaned with annoyance. Mollie Hubbard owned the gaudy villa further down the steep slope of the hill, which unfortunately made her his near neighbour. His *only* neighbour.

After a month in the German hospital near the military base

Max had been granted three months' convalescent leave to recover fully from the injuries inflicted by an explosion activated by a soldier suffering from post-traumatic stress disorder. Clare Goodey owned the sizeable villa in a popular Spanish resort as part of her divorce settlement, and she had insisted on installing him there with a stack of books, his favourite CDs and enough food in the fridge freezer to keep even the most avid trencherman satisfied.

She had spent the first five days at the villa, sitting with him quietly reading or listening to music. His broken jaw had been successfully repaired in Germany, but extended conversation had been best avoided at that early stage in his recovery. His broken arm was still in plaster, which had prevented him from using the swimming pool that beckoned so enticingly. The sight of Clare in a swimsuit partially compensated, while at the same time filling him with natural male urges. The two chipped vertebrae caused him no problem, it was the chest wound which had kept him so long at half strength – something that would have any naturally vigorous man chafing at the bit.

Clare had arranged for him to attend the local hospital to have the plaster removed and his arm X-rayed when what he regarded as his penance was due to end. She had flown over to supervise this, and had remained for three days to ensure he did not do too much too soon. That first time in the pool with her had intensified his longings, but had tired him so much he had been forced to bow to the reality of the punishment his body had taken on the day that haunted his waking hours.

Over and over he told himself he should have guessed what Knott intended to do, and prevented him. The traumatized man would still be alive and receiving the help he had needed. Such a tragic waste of a brave, talented soldier. Thanks to Clare, in her dual role of caring woman and doctor, his illogical sense of guilt had gradually eased and they were tentatively exploring a new state of what had been a casual friendship between neighbours and professional colleagues.

Max, widowed after a two-year marriage and Clare, recently

divorced from a wealthy playboy Guards officer, were taking the altered relationship very slowly, so Max's injuries were not the only reason why they had occupied separate bedrooms during Clare's visits – a fact Mollie Hubbard had unfortunately been aware of.

Being experienced enough in both his private and professional lives to recognize a predatory divorcée set on snaring a new sexual partner, Max had tried every repelling tactic without success. Initially, he had been unable to leave the villa, so a precedent had been set by the determined Mollie who had visited whenever she wished and set herself up as his carer, immune to even the broadest hints.

Once he was able to drive to the village for a meal, or for a drink in the bar run by a former paratrooper and his local girlfriend, Mollie had invariably appeared. Short of being unforgivably rude, Max had been unable to rid himself of the forty-five-year-old who believed she was still in the first flush of youth and irresistible.

Now here she was walking in on his departure preparations. He had reserved a seat on the afternoon flight to Germany, and the plan had been to slip away leaving a farewell note for her to receive once he was well away. There was no chance to pretend he was out; the hire car was there in the car port.

Having rattled the knocker on the front door, the wretched woman was coming to the rear of the property, where the pool Max had used an hour ago gleamed in the noonday sun. Next minute, he heard her usual girlish, 'Cooee' coming from the large open plan ground floor.

Gritting his teeth he descended the stone staircase, looking at his watch with a worried expression. 'Mollie!' he said crisply, 'I had a call from Germany. A life or death situation. Extremely hush-hush, of course. I'm the only person they'll negotiate with and the sand's running out for the hostage.' He took her arm in a strong clasp and walked her back out to the patio. 'They're sending an armed helicopter to pick me up within the hour. I know I can trust you to keep this under your hat and invent a suitable lie to tell everyone here explaining my swift departure, because this concerns national security. Thanks for all your kindness. I'll never forget it.'

That last sentence was true enough, he thought, and he returned to the bedroom and his packing, first entering the bathroom to wipe the lipstick from his mouth and cheeks. Dear God, what a sad woman! He pitied the next innocent male she fastened on. She would doubtless be in the bar tonight repeating word for word the yarn he had spun, revelling in the attention she would get.

Approaching the airport an hour later, Max chuckled. No sign of the armed helicopter arriving to pick him up! With a surge of gladness he relished the prospect of being back in his apartment tonight; back to the life he thrived on. Two weeks of his leave remained, but he felt ready and fit enough to resume command of 26 Section and become involved in the cases presently ongoing. With luck, there would be something meaty to get his teeth into.

TWO

After a very bumpy flight the aircraft arrived ten minutes ahead of schedule. By the time Max collected his two bags and secured a taxi, it was almost twenty-one thirty. Half an hour to reach his apartment, but it would still be a reasonable time to call Tom for news of the state of play, and to explain to Clare why he had come home.

In truth, he would prefer to leave that last until the morning, but she would be aware of someone moving around in his rooms and investigate. She had been keeping an eye on the place during his extended absence.

Once he was back to normal routine the question of deciding the true nature of their relationship would have to be settled, and he was still unsure what that was. With the pain of Livya Cordwell's rejection still hovering, he had no intention of rushing into an affair and risking a repetition. Half inclined to chicken out and take a hotel room for the night, Max decided to give Mollie Hubbard's behaviour as his reason for leaving the villa, saying nothing about how keen he was to be with Clare again. That should keep things neutral for a week or so.

His spirits lifted on sighting the two-storey building which contained two identical apartments separated by a communal large sitting and dining room for entertaining. It was the only home he had, there not having been a family one since his mother died when he was six. Andrew Rydal had sold up and lived in officers' messes around the world while his only son was a boarder in schools, university and then the Army.

Max understood why his father had preferred to live in military quarters on being widowed. He, himself, had done the same after his two-year marriage to Susan had ended with her death in a car crash, but he had lost his own son with her that day. His heady recent romance with his father's ADC had set Max yearning for a real home and children, but Lyvia had wanted those same things with her charismatic boss. She was continuing to work for Andrew even though he had married again very unexpectedly last year, content with no more than the crumbs from his table. Max thought she was surely exacerbating the wound.

Clare's car was not in its spot beside his own. Max was not certain whether to be glad or sorry, but told himself the problem of explaining had been solved for him. If she returned later he would be in bed with the apartment in darkness, and she would have no idea he was there until tomorrow morning.

After a three-month absence his rooms had that stale air of non-occupation, so he threw open the rear windows while downing a large whisky as he unpacked his clothes. It was good to be back, even if there was nothing to eat in the fridge freezer. He had slept through the meal service on the flight – not a great miss, probably – but he felt in need of some kind of sustenance so he opened a tin of corned beef and sandwiched thick slices smeared with mustard between cream crackers from an unopened packet. Weird, but better than nothing.

While he sat chewing the last mouthful, he punched in the number of the landline to Tom's rented house within easy reach of the base. Nora answered, and sounded glad to hear from him.

'Max! How are you? I guess it's a damn sight warmer down there where you are than it is here at the moment.' Then, as if she suddenly realized how late it was, she asked, 'Is everything all right?'

'Never better. I flew in an hour ago.'

'You're home?'

'And raring to go. Everything OK with you and the girls?'

'Fine.'

'How about the little lad? Almost ready to join the Blackies, isn't he?'

'I'll be glad when he does. He's much too lively. Soon as I sit quietly he decides to try his footballing skills.'

Max laughed. 'He needs all the practice he can manage if he takes after his father. Tom couldn't score a goal if the net was a mile wide.'

She also laughed. 'He's always preferred rugger. I'll tell him you're back. He's taking a shower ready for an early night after a call out at three this morning.'

'Oh? Something serious under way?'

'He'll tell you about it tomorrow, Max.'

'Max on the line at this hour?' asked Tom in the background. 'Is he OK?'

'He's come home,' Nora told him, followed by more in an undertone that Max could not translate, but could guess at. She wanted her tired husband to get to bed.

'Had enough of the lotus-eating life among dark-eyed senoritas?' quipped Tom, taking over from Nora.

'If only,' he returned. 'All I attracted was a desperate Irish divorcée of mature years who wanted to eat me for breakfast. I managed to escape whole, but only just. Tom, why the early call this morning?'

An obvious hesitation before, 'You're on leave for two more weeks yet.'

'I'll be at Section Headquarters at the usual time tomorrow morning, so gen me up now and it'll save time then.'

After further hesitation Tom offered a brief account of the charge against Piercey.

'Where is he now?'

In a spare room in the Mess until his own has been combed and declared clean, or until he can produce a solid alibi.'

'Bloody fool,' snapped Max. 'He behaved completely out of character with that woman, but Phil's not a violent man. He'd never assault her because she turned him down. She's protecting someone. Her story has yawning holes in it. We can soon tear that apart.'

'*We?*' There was a definite protest in that one word.

'Tom, I'm perfectly fit and well, I'm back on base and the defendant is a man I trust and value as a member of my team. Of course it's *we*. See you at eight on the dot.'

He took a shower, then lay in bed in the darkness reviewing all he had been told. Tom had twice wanted Piercey posted elsewhere, could not accept the Cornish sergeant's freelance attitude to the job, but Max thought he was nevertheless an asset to the team and overruled Tom. He might have to change his mind after this. Piercey was the last man he would have expected to become so besotted with a woman she would have enough ammunition to charge him with something so serious.

He settled for sleep thanking Mollie Hubbard for driving him back here at exactly the right time.

But for the alarm clock Max would have overslept. When the loud buzzing brought him awake it was a moment or two before he knew where he was, then he gave a delighted grin. Back in command with an interesting case to pursue.

The grin faded when he spotted the envelope propped against the toaster in the small kitchen. The last time that had happened he had read Livya's apology for not loving him the way he believed she did.

This note had not been there last night, which meant Clare had somehow discovered he was back and had come in while he was asleep. He stared at his name written in her typical medic's scrawl. Had she jumped the gun to make it clear her interest in him was just that of a doctor, a neighbour, a professional colleague?

He made coffee and drank a mugful before pulling out the single sheet of notepaper bearing a message that restored the grin.

> I made my usual Sunday inspection to be sure all was as it should be, and found a squatter had moved in. Gave me a fright to see a body in the bed. I have an early start in the morning. Conference at Regional Headquarters. Confess why you returned early over dinner at Herr Blomfeld's. My treat.

There was a large X beneath Clare's name, which made Max's grin widen with pleasure. That inn beside the river where he rowed most Sunday mornings had become 'their place'. Maybe it was fortunate that she was occupied all day. She was unable to stop him from returning to work.

The guard on the main gate greeted him jovially and looked set to embark on a long conversation regarding the explosion that had killed a brave but shattered man and injured Max, but he skilfully escaped and headed for Section Headquarters with his spirits rising by the minute.

The parking area was full. Tom must have put the word around to ensure the team arrived early. There was no mistaking their pleasure because he was back to full fitness, but Max detected a downbeat mood even as they offered him coffee and one of the sultana and walnut muffins he liked so much.

Tom opened the briefing by outlining details of his interview with Maria Norton the previous afternoon, which she had ended abruptly by feigning the onset of illness.

'I'll have another session with her this morning, get the answers to a number of questions I was prevented from asking by the orderly who responded to her cries for assistance. I'll also discover if she tells the same version of events today.'

He looked around at the intent expressions. 'One thing is certain. Captain Goodey told me Norton is in the early stages of pregnancy. That opens an entirely new avenue of possibilities. A more likely one, in my view. The Doc put it in a nutshell. Norton tells the father, he says get rid of it, she says no, he beats her up to make his point.'

'Then she protects him by accusing Phil,' mused Connie Bush. 'Sounds familiar. Remember Sharmayne Parker a few years ago? Accused her husband of knocking her about and was believed, until it happened again when he was on remand at his regimental headquarters. Even when we arrested and charged her lover, she tried to defend him. Crazy woman!'

'Damn near finished Jack Parker's career,' recalled Tom, 'which is why we have to get Piercey off the hook for this, pronto.'

Olly Simpson glanced up from his doodling. 'How do we

do that? Everyone we spoke to yesterday mentioned Phil's obsession with Norton throughout rehearsals, and at the party. He, himself, admits to having a hot session with her backstage, but can't prove he didn't do what she claims.'

Tom gave him a pointed look. 'Then *you* have to find the means to prove it. Someone on this base must have seen him returning to his room that night, or noticed that his car was parked outside the Sergeants' Mess when he says it was. It's not enough to prove he was actually inside the building and in his room, but I'd feel happier about dismissing Norton's version of what happened if we had some solid fact to back it up.'

Derek Beeny, Piercey's friend and frequent investigating partner, asked cautiously, 'You think he might be guilty, sir?'

'I didn't say that, but I'm pretty damn certain he's being economical with the truth over how far he went with Norton in her dressing room. We need a revised statement from him on that.'

'How far he went was as far as she drove him to, you bet,' said Heather Johnson, surprisingly rising to the defence of the man whose personality frequently clashed with hers. 'All the women in the cast that we interviewed yesterday afternoon said she was a right tease, playing off the men against each other.'

'And *they*,' added Connie, 'excused her behaviour as "getting fully into her role".'

Heather scowled. 'Pathetic! Phil might have been as gullible as the rest, but he's too arrogant to beat a woman up if she's reluctant. He'd walk away and find someone more willing. Knowing him, it wouldn't take long.'

Max could see Tom was irritated by this sexist interlude and was not surprised when he interrupted it somewhat forcefully. 'So we know who didn't do it. Let's find who did. I want you all to look at your notes and come up with the names of whichever of your interviewees could have been in the auditorium just before Bill Jensen locked the Recreation Centre. Two men chatting up some chorus girls, according to

Norton. We need to hear their versions of what happened to send Piercey slipping through the rear stage door after Norton ran out there claiming he was trying to strip her. She told me those two men were set to square up to him, and subsequently offered to drive her to her billet.'

'What I don't get,' put in Olly Simpson still gnawing the bone, 'is why this woman who tingled every male's toes, if not elsewhere, had not had offers galore for a romantic tête à tête after the party ended. Why was she lingering in the theatre with just Phil and some guys chatting to chorus girls, unless she'd planned it that way?'

Connie gave him a straight look. 'No romantic offers because the guys with tingling toes had their wives or girlfriends with them at the party. Had to behave themselves.'

'And there's another thing,' added Heather. 'I find it hard to believe the pair who arranged to give her a lift would drive away leaving her there, as she claims. When she went back to look for whatever she reckoned she'd left in the dressing room, and was away for so long, one of them would surely have gone to see if she was OK. If it had happened at a disco in town, and they were all legless, I can see a couple of likely lads telling a taxi driver to get going without her, but this was different.'

Tom nodded. 'A cock and bull story which she must know we'll swiftly demolish. I don't believe her mother called on her mobile to ask about the success of the final performance. Not at that hour, unless Mrs Norton lives in Australia or some place well east of here.'

Max had been sitting quietly listening to this sound reasoning and now had a good grasp of the case. 'I'd like to applaud the importance of finding that group remaining in the theatre when everyone else had left,' he said, entering the discussion. 'Their evidence could swing this case in a new direction. Discovering who made her pregnant is also very important. Captain Goodey's nutshell makes sense. We need to talk to Norton's friends and colleagues about who she's been dating, on or off the base. The pregnancy could be the outcome of a one-night stand after binge drinking in town, of course, which would make it well nigh impossible for us to trace her sexual partner. If he was a local German it would rule out the nutshell theory, because he wouldn't have been on the base at midnight on Saturday.'

Getting into his stride, he continued. 'We also have to explore an angle not yet mentioned. The theatre occupies just one area of the Recreation Centre complex. Any number of activities are catered for, classes in almost any subject under the sun. Check what else was regularly taking place on the same evening as rehearsals for the opera. It's possible that a man pursuing some other hobby saw Norton week after week strutting her stuff in seductive manner and became fixated on her as Carmen.

'It might be a mistake to concentrate too much on a connection between the attack and her pregnancy. Bill Jensen will have details of everything that takes place at the Centre, and we also need his account of that final half hour before he locked the doors after the party.'

Getting to his feet, he nodded at Beeny and Simpson. 'I want you two to concentrate on tracing a witness who'll give Phil an alibi for the actual time of the attack.'

'We don't know the exact time, sir,' Beeny returned somewhat coolly. 'All we have to go on so far is her arrival at the RMP Post at oh two hundred. Her engineered spell of distress prevented Mr Black from questioning her on how the attack ended, and how she managed to reach the Post in that state.'

This pointed reminder that he had picked up on a case that was already one day old made Max aware that his eagerness to get back in harness was not particularly politic. The team had been focussing on Tom, seeing their convalescent boss as merely 'sitting in' at the briefing. Tom had been commanding the Section successfully for four months. Realizing tardily that Tom might resent his trying to take over, Max told himself he must ease his return to full command.

'That's a very pertinent point,' he said quietly. 'Her claim of a call from her mother on the mobile suggests she had it with her after Phil left the theatre. The RMP Post is as far across the base as one can get, so why didn't Norton use the mobile to call for help?'

'It was lost during the assault,' Beeny reasoned.

'Or?' prompted Tom, with a complicit glance at Max.

'The attack took place just a short distance from the Post,' said Connie, picking up the significance of the question. 'Someone *did* give her a lift, and things turned nasty.'

'Which makes our prime object to trace the two men chatting to chorus girls. Where did they disappear to, by the way, leaving the lads free to offer Norton a lift? Did she go with them in good faith then discover they wanted the same as Phil?'

'She'd have been lucky to get away from two men without being raped,' Heather reasoned, 'so I'd say it's more likely that the driver dropped the other man off, then tried his luck with Norton who somehow managed to get away and reach the RMP Post.'

Seeing that Max had sat down again, suggesting he would play no further part in the briefing, Tom wound up the proceedings.

'Trace these two men and the girls who were with them. If you have doubts about the blokes don't hesitate to bring them in for in-depth sessions. Get from Babs Turvey any info on Norton's mobile. It wasn't on the locker beside her bed, and Captain Goodey made no mention of it being with her bagged clothes. Finding it might give us a lead on who she planned to meet after the party, because surely that's why she lingered there so late. If I learn anything new this morning, I'll pass it on.'

Once they were alone, Max apologized. 'You've been running the Section famously in my absence, Tom. I didn't mean to undermine your authority; just spoke my thoughts.' He smiled. 'Too long out of the job; too anxious to get back on board. It's an intriguing case. If Norton continues to blame Piercey you might consider sending Connie to talk to her, woman to woman. That was a valid point from Olly. If the woman's so popular with men why wasn't she inundated with offers to run her home . . . with the hope of being asked in for coffee? Doesn't add up.'

'And a valid point from Connie,' said Tom still somewhat coolly. 'Male admirers were mostly hampered by the presence of wives or girlfriends at the party, and the other women in the cast had no time for her. Seems Norton's lacking female friends.'

'Mmm, she has NCO status, so her work must be satisfactory, but is there a problem with how she uses her rank with her colleagues?'

'Could be. She has a high opinion of herself. Your suggestion of a possible voyeur on rehearsal nights is worth following. She was highly voluptuous as Carmen. Enough to get any guy worked up.'

'Like Piercey. The most significant factor is why she was deliberately lingering in the theatre after the end of the party. If she wasn't chasing Phil she must have arranged to meet someone outside the Recreation Centre after the place was locked up.' He took up his car keys and prepared to leave. 'I'll call on Phil. Talk to him man to man. I'll let you have any useful info that might emerge from that.' Heading for the door, he added, 'I'm having dinner with Clare tonight, doubtless to be given a bollocking for returning early without consulting her. I'll be keen to hear your progress in the morning.' He hesitated before stepping outside. 'It's good to be back where I belong.'

Tom nodded. 'Until you've been passed fit to resume command by the Medical Board, any thoughts on the case will be very welcome.'

Max found Piercey doing press-ups in a spare room in the Sergeants' Mess. After initial surprise at seeing his Section Commander, who was thought to be in Spain for another fortnight, the accused sergeant looked relieved.

'It's good to see you've fully recovered, sir. Please come in. I'll slip on some clothes, then make coffee.'

'This isn't a social call, Phil,' Max told him. 'Forget the coffee. I'm here to get to the bottom of this deplorable business you're involved in.'

The smile vanished as Piercey registered Max's official tone, and he snatched from the bed blue jog pants and a sweatshirt to pull on over his colourful boxer shorts. Sweeping a pile of magazines from a chair he invited his boss to sit on it.

'I read your statement at Headquarters a short while ago. It varies considerably from the version of events Corporal Norton gave Mr Black, so I'm here to get from you the truth. If we are to defend you, we have to have the facts. You know that, man. It's your profession. But you're in danger of losing all that unless we can prove you're innocent of this serious charge.'

'I am. That *is* the truth.'

'I don't doubt it, but let's have the revised version of your encounter in Norton's dressing room, leaving nothing out this time.'

Max then heard how Maria Norton had led him to believe she fancied him, then did the same to someone else in his presence at every rehearsal.

'She really got to me like no girl has before,' he confessed quietly. 'I kidded myself she behaved that way to keep everything chilled while we were engaged with the opera. She's good,' he said fervently. 'Should be singing professionally. The Army's wrong for her.'

'She wears two stripes. It can't be too wrong for her. How did the other men react to her capriciousness?'

Piercey shrugged. 'Same as me, I imagine. Looked forward to the last-night party and hoped she'd give us what we'd wanted for the past two months.'

'You expected to have sex with her that night?'

'She'd been promising it for eight weeks.'

Max frowned. 'She actually said she'd go to bed with you after the party?'

'Well, as good as. Each time I suggested it she said I should "tie a knot in it" until the show ended and she could relax. I took that as a promise.'

'Good God, man, surely you're too experienced to fall for that.'

'Yes, I am, but she made it really obvious she wanted it as much as I did.'

'When? Where were you both when she made it so obvious?'

'Just beyond the stage door. It was hot in the theatre so she used to go outside during a short period she wasn't on stage, to cool down before her dying scene.' He hesitated before continuing with an account he would prefer to keep to himself. 'I used to slip away from that choral session to join her. I suppose she was still acting when she teased me. You know, running her hands over my tight satin breeches, saying I must be patient until the final performance.'

Max well understood the provocation, but he was still surprised that this dedicated womaniser had succumbed so fully. He was even more surprised to see the healthy flush colour Piercey's cheeks in a rush of embarrassment.

'So did you have an arrangement with her to take her somewhere when the party ended?'

'I booked a room at the Black Bear, intending to drive her there as a surprise.'

'It wasn't a mutual plan?'

'No.' The outcome of that night appeared to hit Piercey once more, and he looked defeated. 'I bought a bottle of perfume to give her to show how much I admired her performance, then I waited for everyone to leave and went to her dressing room to give it to her and reveal where we'd be spending the night.'

It was almost unnecessary for him to describe what happened. Max could guess how it went, but he had to hear it in Piercey's own words.

'Go on.'

After a deep sigh the sorry tale spilled out. 'She was taking a call on her mobile. I went up behind her, put my arms around her, and kissed her on the neck. She shrugged me away; told whoever she was talking to she'd call back in ten. I said she'd have to make it the next morning because she was going to be too occupied to make phone calls. That's when I sprung the surprise about the Black Bear.' Piercey gazed down at his linked hands, clearly unhappy over what he must tell this man who was an officer and his boss, as well as someone he liked and trusted.

'She laughed. Said, "In your dreams, Phil," and turned away. I . . . well, I suppose I lost it for a moment or two. The zip on her dress was undone, so I pulled it from her shoulders and decided to have a taste of what I'd been promised.' Another deep sigh. 'I was pretty insistent.'

'You tried to strip her?'

Piercey shook his downbent head. 'The costume had a built-in bra, so her breasts were bared.'

'You handled them?'

'Briefly, but the dress tore as she tried to pull it back in place. That's when I stopped and stepped away from her. Next minute she's running out front shouting that I was trying to get her naked.' He glanced up then. 'I decided to cut my losses and left by the stage door.'

'Mmm, I won't comment on the wisdom of that. Where did you go?'

'Came back here. Should've gone to the Black Bear. The staff could've given me an alibi.' He frowned. 'She'd touched me sexually often enough. I only responded in kind. No way would I beat her up.'

'Well, Norton is claiming you came out of the darkness and began slapping and punching her. You must see that it would be easy to believe a man who had been publicly humiliated after being promised sexual intercourse would be angry enough to lay in wait to punish the woman in some way.' Max paused before continuing. 'Philip Piercey, did you wait outside the Recreation Centre and violently assault Maria Norton?'

The other man gazed unwaveringly back at Max. 'No, sir, I did not.'

After a moment or two, Max nodded. 'You'll have to submit a more accurate statement based on what you've just told me. We'll get you out of the frame as soon as possible. Meanwhile, you'll remain suspended from duty and confined to barracks.' He smiled. 'I'll now have that coffee you offered me, Phil.'

THREE

After Max left, Tom had a rethink and called Connie Bush to tell her to meet him outside the Medical Centre. Norton might, indeed, respond more willingly with a woman present. Ostensibly, Connie would be there to take down the victim's statement, but if Norton tried the same trick to halt the questioning, Connie was capable of calming the situation and taking over from Tom.

They were met with the news that Corporal Norton was no longer there. The duty orderly told Tom the MO had agreed to allow the patient to rest in her own quarters, but to attend Sick Parade on Thursday to check progress. 'She's excused duty for seven days, sir.'

'When did she go?'

'She left right after breakfast, sir.'

'So why didn't you inform me? You're aware that SIB is investigating the serious assault which put her in your care.'

The orderly's face remained expressionless. 'There was no instructions left on that, sir.'

Highly irritated, Tom snapped, 'Are you incapable of making decisions? If a patient had a sudden relapse in the MO's absence would you let him die because she hadn't left instructions to resuscitate him? God help all ye who enter herein!'

Back beside their vehicles Tom told Connie to follow him to the accommodation block housing Maria Norton. 'We'll have better luck there, anyway. She can't call for medication if the questions grow awkward.'

When they reached the room at the far end of the first floor corridor they found it unoccupied. The wardrobe door stood open revealing empty hangers; there were no shoes on the rack.

'She's done a runner,' declared Connie, indicating two empty drawers in the bedside locker.

'What the hell game is that woman playing?' breathed Tom, now certain there were greater depths to this case than was first thought. Max would relish the fact.

Heather struck gold at her second attempt to trace one of the men Norton claimed had offered her a lift. Lance Corporal Roy Broderick had been in the chorus of *Carmen*, he was twenty-two and single, which made him a likely candidate. He had been off base yesterday and had therefore not yet been interviewed. He was in the gymnasium directing a workout routine for an infantry platoon when Heather located him, and he reluctantly left his class to continue without his supervision while they went to his office.

Blond and beefy, he earned Heather's well-hidden appreciation of his muscles while she marvelled that he could also sing well enough for opera. Much the same as Piercey, of course.

'I suppose it's about Maria Norton,' he began in a voice overlaid with similar Cornish inflections as there were in Piercey's. 'I heard she was beaten up by your colleague.'

'Then you heard wrong,' she countered.

'Oh?' He stood feet apart, hands on hips in a semi-confrontational pose. 'How's that, then?'

Ignoring this challenge, she got straight to the point. 'What time did you leave the theatre after the party on Saturday night, Corporal?'

'When I was chucked out by Bill Jensen, Sarge,' he replied with a patronizing grin.

Facing him with an unflinching stare, she said, 'Let's get this straight before we go any further. In the early hours of Sunday morning a woman you had acted in company with for two months was viciously assaulted. She has given us a state-ment which suggests you can offer evidence which could help us to apprehend whoever was responsible for her injuries, so let's be grown up and take this investigation into a major crime seriously. What time did you leave the theatre, Corporal?'

His blue eyes lost their amused sparkle. 'Must've been around one fifteen. I wasn't watching the clock.'

'Was anyone with you when you left?'

'Yes.'

'Give me their names,' she said, knowing he was going to be as awkward as possible in retaliation.

'Chancer Blakey and two girls he brought to the party.'

'Rank and real name of Blakey?'

'Lance Corporal, Morgan.'

'And the girls?'

'Manda and Jess. That's all I know apart from they're daughters of guys in Afghanistan right now. Sixth form schoolgirls.'

So Norton was wrong about their being in the chorus. A glance at her list of the cast of *Carmen* showed Blakey as having a very minor solo role as a gypsy. Turning away from Broderick, Heather called Beeny's mobile and told him to seek out Blakey as the second of the pair Norton mentioned. She deliberately ended by arranging to meet up with him later to see how the evidence offered by the two compared.

Broderick was aggressive and had resumed his confrontational pose when she turned back to him.

'Look, what's going down here? Chancer and me aren't bloody suspects for this. *He* tried it on backstage with her. Stands to reason he had another go at her when she left.'

Against a background of thumps, bumps and laughter from the soldiers continuing their gymnastics, Heather asked, 'We're talking about Maria Norton, are we? Tell me about this backstage business you witnessed.'

'No, you're putting words in my mouth. I didn't *witness* anything, but it happened. She ran out to us crying rape.' He caught himself up. 'No, not exactly. She said he was trying to pull her clothes off, and we could see her dress was ripped.'

'Was she frightened, angry, or just disgusted?'

'How the hell do I know what she felt? I was busy trying to make it with these schoolgirls. The way that silly cow had been putting herself about with all the men, she was asking for it.'

Heather had to bite back her withering comment on that favourite male statement. Instead, she asked him what happened when Maria joined him, Blakey and the girls.

'Chancer had put a fair bit away during the party, so had the girls, come to that, and he started bragging that he'd sort the bugger out. Trying to impress them, see. They egged him on, but I talked sense to him. He's up for promotion to full corporal. Having a go at one of you lot would put an end to that.'

'I see. So there was no attempt by any of you to go backstage to confront Sergeant Piercey?'

He shook his head. 'Chancer carried on growling about it, but your mate chickened out by leaving through the stage door, the girls were going on about how late it was, and Bill Jensen was rattling his bunch of keys, so we left.'

'And Maria?'

'Last we saw of her she was heading backstage again, calling to Bill that she had a quick call on her mobile to make and she wouldn't be long.'

'You didn't offer her a lift?'

'She had her own transport. Saw it in the car park as we drove off.'

Excited by what she was being told, Heather asked, 'Any other vehicles still there?'

'Only Jensen's clapped-out Volvo.'

So, witnesses to the fact that Phil had driven away from the Centre! Not electrifying, but it was a start. All that was needed now was confirmation that his vehicle had arrived outside the Sergeants' Mess and remained there during the vital period.

Broderick was showing his impatience to return to directing his class. 'Is that it, then?'

'Where did you go after leaving the theatre?'

'Took the girls home.'

'Without stopping en route?' she asked caustically.

He gave the cheeky grin again. 'No need. Manda's mum is a fun-loving woman. We continued the party at her place until the neighbours began thumping on the wall.'

'What time was that?'

The grin developed into a chuckle. 'She had one of those Swiss cuckoo clocks. It cuckooed three times as we were leaving. We were all pissed enough by then to cuckoo outside the neighbours' window until their bedroom light came on. Then we scarpered.'

'Pity,' thought Heather. Too late for them to have witnessed Norton's struggle to reach the RMP Post. However, Broderick had shed light on some new slants. There had been no offer of a lift, Norton had her own means of getting wherever she intended to go after her phone call, she had made a call on her mobile before she left the Centre – it would be valuable to know to whom – and she had been left there alone with Bill Jensen. Did that make him a suspect?

Leaving the gymnasium, Heather sat in her car to review all she knew about Bill Jensen. Retiring as a senior warrant officer, part of whose responsibility was management of the Recreation Centre, Bill had applied to continue doing just that as a civilian. He was married to a German ballet teacher who owned a house in town, and he was interested in the Arts. His application had been approved. He still ran the Centre and was still regarded by those who used it as a formidable sergeant major. It worked well.

Heather knew him as a man of principle, well liked and respected, but one never could tell what lay beneath a person's facade and he had been alone with a promiscuous young woman wearing a torn dress in the early hours. Had Bill watched Maria night after night in the guise of Carmen and lusted after her? He was of an age when many men felt driven to prove their virility was not waning. The one question mark in that theory was why Norton would accuse Phil Piercey in order to protect a man old enough to be her father.

At that stage in her thoughts her friend Connie called to tell her Maria Norton had absconded. Using their pet name for Tom, she added, 'Blackie's trying to decide if this action is equivalent to withdrawing her charge against Phil. He's busy studying regs to find out.'

'No need for that, just ask the Boss. He'll know. He's also itching to get back in the saddle, and I'd feel happier if he resumed command rather than mooch about on the sidelines. My gran maintains there's nothing worse than a man dithering about with not enough to occupy him, and I agree with her. Let's work on it.'

Olly Simpson was gradually working down the list of people living in the block overlooking the Sergeants' Mess parking area. A number had been absent yesterday on a weekend pass or on a Sunday excursion. There were four men still to be approached when the person he was questioning added complications which were unwelcome.

They were standing in a massive clothing store where Private 'Jimmy' James worked for Headquarter Company. A man in his thirties who had never earned promotion, he was content with his lot, as he explained before Simpson could put the vital questions.

'Did an apprenticeship with a firm of bespoke tailors, Sarge, but never got no further than rolling up the cloth shown to the customers and putting them back in the cabinets. I took a pride in them never having a crease or a crumple when they was next unrolled along the counter. Immaculate they was. And I always stacked them according to colours and shades of colours. Mr McAuley often sang my praises, saying as how the shop looked so smart and orderly it lured in even those gentlemen who were most fastidious.

'I used to deliver the items in the liveried van, if the customer didn't want to carry them away when finished. I enjoyed that. Saw some posh houses if they asked me to step inside.' He grinned. 'Usually got a tip. More than tuppence, I can tell you.'

Bored with this second day of interviewing, Simpson let the man ramble on and eventually asked why he had left the job he so enjoyed.

'Ah well, seeing all those grand houses and overhearing what the gentlemen said to Mr Parkes, the fitter, it struck me that I ought to see some of them foreign places they operated in. So I enlisted.' He waved an arm at the shelves bearing every item of kit a soldier needed. 'Got the best of both worlds, haven't I? Seeing Germany where me grandad fought, way back, and I can lay me finger on any item in here quicker than three minutes. What more could I ask for?'

'With that kind of attention to detail you might be the person SIB is looking for,' Simpson told him.

'No, Sarge, I don't think I'd like policing.'

Unsure whether to be amused or insulted by this stolid man's misapprehension, Simpson said, 'As a witness, man. Did you happen to notice Sergeant Piercey return to the Sergeants' Mess late on Saturday night?'

James beamed. 'It was more like Sundee morning. See, I enjoy watching the late night TV film on Satdee. Then, because it's nearly always violent or a horror movie, I go out for a little walk round before turning in. Can't sleep otherwise. Film ends just after one and I plan to walk for around fifteen minutes, so it was as I turned the corner coming back that I saw him drive up and go straight in. Mind you,' he added thoughtfully, 'it was his wheels, but the bloke who got from it was wearing some kind of fancy dress. Can't swear it was him, but he looked the right height and weight.' He nodded wisely. 'I can gauge it very accurately, after being in the business so long.'

'It was him,' Simpson assured him, feeling elated. Phil had an alibi!

'Then he went out again ten minutes later.'

'What?'

James nodded. 'Saw from my window the car being backed out. Then it speeded off around the perimeter road. Came here to change, I s'pose. Wherever he was going he was in a bleeding hurry.'

Piercey was about to call Beeny's mobile to suggest they meet in the NAAFI for a snack lunch, when there was a knock and his door opened.

'Come to escort me when I go to eat?' he jokingly asked his colleague.

'You'll notice I'm not smiling,' said Simpson curtly. 'The

entire team's out seeking a witness who can give you an alibi.
I've just found one, but he turns out to be a witness for the
prosecution.'

Piercey frowned. 'What's that supposed to mean?'

'There's no suppose about it, Phil. It means what I said.'

Piercey's temper rose. 'A lying witness! I *didn't* beat her
up.' He had just been forced to reveal to his boss some intimate
details of his passionate response to Maria's callous rejection
and now wanted to draw a veil over that business in the dressing
room, but Olly was raking it up again. 'Who is this witness?'

Simpson perched on the small desk. 'A certain Private James
of HQ Company, who lives opposite you. He saw you arrive
there in your Spanish outfit.'

'Great!' he exclaimed. 'Can he pinpoint the time?'

'Almost to the minute.'

'There you are, then,' he crowed, getting up from his chair.
'I'm off the hook, mate.'

'He then saw you go out again ten minutes later.'

'*What*?' He flung out his arm. 'I sat on my bed and made
inroads to a six-pack until Babs and Jeff arrived. Maria dobbed
me in to protect someone. I suppose I can understand that,
but why should this HQ bloke also point the finger?' Pushing
a hand through his hair in agitation, he asked, 'How can he
have seen me leave when I didn't? Tell me that.'

Looking uneasy, Simpson said, 'He claims to have seen
your Audi go off hell for leather along the perimeter road.'

'He mistook it for another vehicle.'

'No, he saw the one you drove in being backed from that
same parking bay ten minutes later.'

Feeling as if the breath had been knocked from him, Piercey
slowly lowered himself on the bed. 'Is he prepared to swear
to it?'

'I'm afraid so.'

All thought of going somewhere for a snack vanished as he
sat staring into space. 'That evidence won't exactly put me in
the frame. He's saying I was out in my car during the vital
period, that's all. It won't prove I committed the assault.'

'They'll find your DNA all over her clothes,' Simpson pointed out quietly.

'And the DNA of whoever did it.'

'His, too, but they won't have him to make a comparison with.'

'The way they can with me,' he murmured heavily. 'God, I wish I'd never met that bloody woman.'

'The cry of many a despairing man.' Simpson allowed a short pause before asking, 'Phil, did you go out again?'

'No.' If it sounded less than vehement it was because his thoughts were racing. 'Someone hijacked my car. I was so worked up when I left the theatre I couldn't get to the anonymity of my room fast enough.' He glanced up at his colleague. 'I left the keys in the ignition. Made it easy, didn't I? That James idiot saw the vehicle, but he didn't tell you he saw me get in it, did he?' Simpson's negative shake of his head led him to sigh with satisfaction. 'No, so the Boss'll make short work of any suggestion of involvement based on such vague evidence.' He frowned. 'Unless it was Maria who drove my car away, which is bloody unlikely, there's someone else determined to stitch me up. When Babs and Jeff hauled me off, my car was exactly where I'd left it an hour or so before. They were witnesses to the fact. *Solid* witnesses!' He sighed heavily. 'D'you understand what's behind all this, because I sure as hell don't.'

Before Simpson could reply, his mobile rang. He took a brief call while gazing at Piercey throughout. When it ended, he said, 'That was Connie. Seems Maria Norton has gone, taking all her possessions. The guard at the gate says she drove from the base at around oh nine thirty, then left her car just short of the junction with the autobahn and transferred to a waiting taxi. It took his attention because he thought it was odd behaviour. Her car's being brought in.'

Feeling that he was caught up in some extravagant work of fiction, Piercey said incredulously, 'She's *deserted*?'

'Wardrobe and drawers empty, apparently. I'd say it means she doesn't intend coming back, wouldn't you?'

'But . . . I was told she was so badly hurt she was recovering in the Medical Centre. How can she have . . . ? Olly, she's obviously involved in something beyond her control.'

'Drugs?' Simpson's eyes narrowed. 'I've never met the woman, but you're familiar enough with the signs and knew her intimately. Sorry, wrong word. You'd have read the signs, or were you so dazzled, mate, they passed unnoticed?'

Ignoring the jibe, Piercey shook his head. 'She wasn't a user, but she could well have popped a tab before each performance. I could equate her vitality on stage with a little help from E. She was *electric*.' He remembered his response to her provocation; the response of all the males in the cast. 'You didn't see the show, did you?'

'Not my scene. So, what if she just bought enough to get her through rehearsals and the four performances, then refused to buy more? Or failed to keep up the payments. The pusher beats her up, threatens to leak to us that she's been using on a large scale unless she pays what she owes. She does a runner.'

Piercey shook his head once more. 'Ecstasy's recreational, that's all. Not serious enough for that scenario. Besides, how would that lead the pusher to involve me, because someone took my car, kept it during the significant time of the assault, then returned it before Babs and Jeff arrived to take me in.'

'OK, so use that hypothesis in a different direction, Phil. Norton's injuries couldn't have been self-inflicted, and surely wouldn't have been willingly suffered as part of a plan to damage you, because she's pregnant. So tell me why she named you, and why your car was driven away then returned in the early hours of Sunday morning.'

Piercey stared back at him in cold anger. 'Because I came here to change my stage costume for a dark track suit, then drove back to wait for her to leave the Recreation Centre so I could give her a good going over for treating me like dirt.'

'Exactly.' Simpson slid from his perch on the desk and gave a faint smile. 'Luckily, your victim has scarpered, so we can't take her charge any further. How about some lunch? There's steak and kidney duff on the menu in the Mess today.'

Tom called in every member of the team, including Piercey, after allowing them time for lunch. After checking regulations he was left feeling intensely irritated. Regardless of the apparent desertion of Corporal Maria Norton, the case against Piercey could not be dropped. An official charge against him had been made and would remain on record until it was fully investigated, or until it was withdrawn. However, there was no reason why the accused man could not perform limited duties while the case was on hold.

Once they had gathered together, Tom listened to what had been learned from those who had been questioned during the morning, and summed up the evidence so far.

'First of all, we have to take on board the fact that much of what Norton told me was untrue or exaggerated, which casts doubt on her accusation. We now have evidence of another person being involved in the events of Saturday night and Sunday morning, when Piercey's car was moved around without his knowledge. There are two obvious explanations. Either it was part of a campaign against him, or someone saw him park the vehicle and decided to borrow it for a purpose in no way connected to the attack on Maria Norton.'

He gave a sour smile. 'At a time when innocent people should be in bed, an amazing number are out and about. The witness to this car-jacking himself admitted to taking a walk to calm himself down after watching the late night movie on Saturdays, so whoever took the car could have had God knows what under way. If, however, it was tied in with Norton that person is a strong suspect for the assault on her. If it was a further move to implicate Piercey we need to investigate in greater depth.

'All in all, I think we can safely reckon this mystery man is living on the base, his ability to move around here in the early hours making that a safe assumption. His knowledge of the layout of an establishment the size of this one strengthens it. Unless he's also gone AWOL we need to get a definite ID on him.'

Heather had been sitting restlessly throughout this summary and now seized the opportunity to say what was on her mind. 'Whatever the reason for taking the vehicle we can surely narrow the identity field somewhat. Chummy could also have witnessed Phil drive up and enter the Mess, in which case he's living in the same block as Jimmy James and would have a clear sight of the mess parking area from his window. Alternatively, he could have arrived there in his own car which he parked around the corner out of sight. If so, our pal from HQ would surely have noticed a vehicle parked in an unlikely place when he took his early morning walk. He needs to be questioned on that.'

Tom nodded. 'And a few others, such as how come he saw the Audi being backed out and driven away, but not who was at the wheel? You can chase him up this afternoon.'

Turning to Connie, he said, 'Give Norton's car a thorough search for anything that gives a clue to places she visits in town, phone numbers of people she regularly contacts, evidence of drugs, any clue to who Chummy might be. I'm going to tackle Bill Jensen. Get his version of what happened after the party on Saturday night, and the details of what else was taking place at the Centre when rehearsals for *Carmen* were under way.'

Several minutes later he was alone with Piercey. 'I want you to set up the usual alerts for AWOL personnel. Norton cleverly transferred to a taxi outside the main gate so that her vehicle reg number couldn't be put on the system, but enter her description and warn all exit points to look out for her. Contact all local taxi firms. Find out where she was dropped off and if she was met by someone who was waiting for her. If there's a sighting of her let me know pronto.'

Taking up his car keys, Tom hesitated before saying, 'Your present status quo is tricky, but I'll do what I can to make it as elastic as possible.'

Piercey nodded slowly. 'Thanks, sir . . . and I apologize for what I said to you earlier.'

'No need. There was an element of truth in it.'

Bill Jensen was not in his office just inside the main door of the large Recreation Centre, so Tom began a search of all the rooms. The first contained several rows of very pregnant women lying flat on rush mats while harp music soothed them. In the next were pre-school children wearing protective overalls splashed with as much paint as the sheets of paper in front of them.

Further along the corridor women dressed in coloured brassiere tops and gaudy skirts were being instructed in belly dancing. Tom shuddered at the sight of a couple of them whose belly could dance without any encouragement. As the Turkish music faded, he came upon a group of four earnest-looking women engrossed in a lecture which the blackboard proclaimed to be on the subject of creative writing.

Of course, daytime use of the Centre was mostly by women and children. Evening functions would be less gender-orientated. Tom smiled to himself at the thought of classes the men would be offered. Beer belly dancing? Creative sex? The correct way to eat Indian takeaways?

Having looked everywhere else in vain, Tom walked through to the theatre. He found his quarry backstage stowing stage costumes in large wicker hampers by little more than half light. Jensen caught sight of him and smiled.

'Long time no see, Tom. Pity it has to be official, but I guessed you'd send someone along here before long.' Leaving his task, he approached waving his arm towards the exit. 'Time for tea and biscuits, I reckon.'

'In a minute, Bill. I want to get a clear assessment of this area. How many dressing rooms are there?'

The other man halted beside him and surveyed the narrow passage running behind the raised stage. 'Six, all told. Four small ones and two a great deal larger for men and women in the chorus. The small ones are used according to what kind of show it is, and who's in it.' His frank brown gaze fastened on Tom. 'Don Jose and Escamillo were content to share, but Carmen demanded her own space. Needed to be alone "to metamorphose into the role" before each performance.'

His tone betrayed his opinion of that affected concept. 'Bit of a madam, was she?'

'Tom, if your man hadn't lost his cool and belted her, there were a coupla others who would've.'

'Anyone in particular?' he asked casually.

Jenson recognized what was happening and grew cautious. 'Young Piercey went too far back here after the party. Entered her dressing room while she was changing and tried to pull her dress off. Ripped it. Fact, Tom.' He indicated the hampers. 'It should be going back to the hire company with the rest, but you lot are keeping it for forensic examination. I'm not sure how to explain why I'm not returning it. These costumes cost a hell of a lot to hire. I guess I'll have to rob the kitty to pay for a replacement.'

'Were you back here when it happened? You saw Piercey do it?'

Jensen's mouth pursed knowingly. 'Closing ranks?'

'How much of what went on after the party were you witness to?'

After short hesitation, Jensen said, 'Let's have that cuppa in my office, Tom,' and headed determinedly in that direction, passing the Turkish dancing, the painting toddlers and expectant mothers before entering his own domain and filling an electric kettle.

Busy pouring milk into two large mugs, he asked over his shoulder, 'You have evidence that puts him in the clear?'

'We have evidence that much of what Norton says is untrue.' Tom had no intention of revealing the state of play in the case. 'It throws doubt on her general veracity.'

Still with his back turned, Jensen came back with, 'I person- ally wouldn't believe a single word that came out of her mouth. Lives in a fantasy world. One in which she's entitled to public worship.' He turned to hand over a mug of tea. 'Mind you, she could sing as well as act. Had a voice to put a tingle up a man's spine.'

'Yours, too?'

'Hey, hey! My wife's a ballet teacher, and we're both considerably involved with the Arts,' he said robustly. 'Don't group me with youngsters who're only considerably involved with *sex*. I gave that opinion as a member of the local municipal choir. I know a good mezzo when I hear one.'

Tom raised his eyebrows. 'What is it with all these soldiers who're suddenly bursting into song?'

Jensen grinned at him over his mug. 'Come on, Tom, troops have through the ages expressed their feelings with a lusty sing-song. Don't tell me you've never bellowed a vulgar chorus to Colonel Bogey.'

'I sure as hell didn't send tingles up men's spines.' He sipped the scalding tea. 'Tell me what happened prior to locking up on Saturday, Bill. What you *actually* saw and heard.'

Jensen sat on a scruffy swivel chair, putting his mug on the bench beside him. 'I spent as much as fifteen minutes persuading loiterers to leave. The celebrations were well and truly over an hour after midnight, but a couple of lads with what looked like schoolgirls done up to seem ten years older were still hanging around by the front row. I told them twice to get going, but they just moved several rows back.'

'Where was Carmen at this time?'

'Still soaking up flattery and red wine up on the stage, with a trio of guys all of whom looked typical likely lads. Your man was hanging around in the wings, waiting for them to go. Both he and La Norton were still in their stage costumes, so I decided enough was enough and called out that I would be locking the place in fifteen minutes flat, so they'd better get changed pdq.'

'Then what?'

'Norton kissed each of her admirers and pushed them provocatively towards the steps leading down to the auditorium. She then left the stage by the rear steps to reach her dressing room. When I glanced in the wings Piercey was no longer there, so I assumed they were both obeying my instruction to get into their own clothes.'

'But they didn't.'

'No. Anyway, I again chivvied the guys with the schoolgirls. Their response was the typical "Yeah, yeah," and I heard one of the girls suggest going to her place because her dad was away and her mum got lonely. It was at that point that I moved to the back of the auditorium intending to check that no one was using other areas for a bit of nookie. That's when I heard Norton shouting and screaming rape. She was clinging to one of the guys and creating merry hell.'

He sighed heavily. 'Time I got down to where she was making the melodramatic most of the situation, the guys were arguing about giving Phil Piercey what for. I saw that her dress was torn, and she kept insisting that he tried to strip her. I headed for the dressing rooms, but there was no one there. I guessed he'd skipped out through the stage door, which only opens from inside. I was glad of that. Last thing I wanted was a heavy set-to. Men fighting over a woman. Fool's game, that.'

Tom nodded his agreement. He had seen it happen often enough to know it rarely solved anything, and often brought misery.

'Well, when I arrived back out front Carmen was alone and looking perfectly composed. I heard the others out in the corridor, making for the exit, so I suggested she grabbed her things and got going too, telling her she should bring the torn costume back in the morning, because I intended to lock up right away. She went backstage saying she must just make a quick call before leaving.'

He shook his head in a bemused gesture. 'A few minutes later I went round to the dressing rooms to hurry her up only to find she'd gone out the same way Piercey had. The stage door was open and swinging in the wind. I was bloody annoyed. No word of thanks or farewell.'

Tom could imagine the chagrin. 'Were there any cars outside when you left?'

'Just mine. She'd bloody gone with the wind, mate.'

'Right.' He finished his tea in one gulp. 'Thanks, Bill. We'll need a written statement from you later, so keep the facts clear in your memory.'

'In case I'm lying?'

'No. It's pretty damn obvious who's lying in this affair. I'll leave you to finish packing away the stage costumes, but I'd like a copy of the list of classes held in the Centre on the same night of the week that rehearsals for *Carmen* took place.'

Jensen looked askance at him. 'I see why you want it, but I tell you now you're going up a creek without a paddle there. Your man Piercey was so enmeshed by that woman you'll never cut him free. It was him, Tom, take my word.'

FOUR

Max arrived early at the inn in case Clare managed to get away before the time she had suggested, but he was still looking for her thirty minutes after her hoped-for ETA. Herr Blomfeld seemed more concerned by her tardiness, and Max began to be irritated by the man's fussing which drove him to seek the peace of the garden bordering the river.

A full moon silvered the smooth water gliding past the wooden tables and benches so well used on summer evenings by local diners, who feasted in true Germanic style with laughter and song. Right now, the silence was broken only by the occasional splash as river creatures went about their nocturnal business. It suited Max's mood.

He had not seen Clare for five weeks and cursed this delay to the meeting he felt would surely tell him where they were heading now he was fully restored to fitness. His heart sank when his mobile began to vibrate in his pocket and he saw the caller was she.

'There's been a multi-vehicle pile-up involving a tanker. It's horrendous, Max. We're likely to be involved here until the early hours. Don't wait up.'

He closed the phone and returned it to his pocket, recalling the first time he had brought Clare here. Their meal had been interrupted when a few hyped-up students had jumped into the river, and during their larking one had almost drowned. Max had gone in to rescue her and Clare had resuscitated her while Blomfeld had called an ambulance. Clare had then spoken an undeniable truth. Doctors and policemen could never put aside what they were no matter where they might be.

Having stocked up with provisions after interviewing Piercey, Max decided that scrambled eggs at home would suffice. In his disappointment he drove away without informing Herr Blomfeld that he would not be using the reserved table.

The planned egg dish was swapped for a double-decker cheese, pickle and tomato sandwich accompanied by several whiskies. At midnight he got into bed. At twelve thirty he got out of it and peered from his window, knowing her car would not be there. He would have heard her drive up and slam the door.

He switched on the TV. A choice of some weird American horror film, or a programme featuring women with gigantic breasts and men with similarly outsized genitals who wanted surgery to make them manageable. Again, it was a US programme with dubbed German voices. Max switched the set off in frustration, feeling sorry for people on night shifts who had such a dire selection to help pass the time.

He went back to bed and was still awake at three o'clock when he heard Clare return. Unable to resist the impulse, he again peered from his window. Then he wished he had not. Climbing from the passenger seat was Major Duncan MacPherson, the Medical Officer of the Drumdorran Fusiliers whose left hand was heavily bandaged. It made sense that the two doctors would have attended the conference together, and the handsome Scot looked to have been hurt during the traffic accident. But not enough to have been hospitalized! Was it absolutely necessary for Clare to bring him to her flat for the night? All Max's earlier worries about MacPherson's interest in her returned to keep him awake until light began to filter through the curtains.

When the alarm buzzed him awake Max saw the incident in a different light and jealousy faded. A large mug of black coffee and an equally large fried breakfast banished introspection and uncertainty about returning to duty before clearance from a medical board. 26 Section was *his* team and a member of it was presently depending on his colleagues to find proof of his innocence of a serious crime. No way was Max going to laze around at home for another two weeks in such circumstances.

Pouring fresh coffee he punched Tom's home number on his handset and waited for him to pick up.

'Morning, Max,' said Nora against a background of young girls' voices. 'If you're wanting Tom, I'm afraid George called him out fifteen minutes ago because some of our personnel were involved in a multi-vehicle crash last night. He'll probably be occupied with that for most of the morning.'

'Right. Bye, Nora.'

Having filled the tank last night and given the vehicle a good run to the riverside inn after four months parked outside his apartment, Max was soon on his way to the base RMP Post, where he knew Tom would be.

Sergeant George Maddox, in command of the uniformed police on the base, was surprised to see Max enter the outer office where he was in conversation with Tom. Surprised and wary. Max greeted them both with deliberate geniality.

'Captain Goodey informed me of the serious RTA last night. She and Major MacPherson were returning from a conference and stayed to help rescue the victims. She wasn't aware of any British casualties.' He addressed George. '*Polizei* contacted you?'

'Yes, sir.'

'How many, and where are they?'

'Three guys. Their Audi was badly burned and blistered, but the number plate was a military one, so they contacted us an hour or so ago. They're all in a private clinic just outside Gründorf. The nearest hospital couldn't cope with the numbers. Had to farm out to several clinics in the vicinity those who weren't in life-threatening conditions. Twelve poor sods didn't make it at the scene. The tanker hit a truck carrying gas cylinders and the lot went up. Boom!'

Realizing what he had said to a man who had recently been injured in an explosion, George's colour rose, but Max just said quietly, 'It was safer when we all travelled on horses. Do we yet know the identity of the three casualties?'

George glanced significantly at Tom, which puzzled Max somewhat. 'I sent Babs Turvey and Jerry Hicks to get identification. One's in a reasonably stable condition – the other two are pretty rough – but he was able to tell us what we wanted to know. The most seriously injured is married. Wife's on her way to the clinic. NOK of the other two are being informed. They're not on the critical list, so it's up to the parents to decide whether to come over or not. They'll have been given the phone number of the clinic to check on their progress.'

'Anything suspicious about their condition?' asked Max. 'No suggestion of terrorist involvement, is there?'

'No, sir,' answered George, again glancing at Tom.

'So why has SIB been called in on a road accident? Not our province, is it?'

After brief hesitation, Tom answered. 'Staff Sergeant Andrews, one of the more serious casualties, is in an induced coma and unable to be questioned, but Babs Turvey searched through all their clothes for personal items and found in his wallet a photograph of himself and a girl with their arms round each other. She's Maria Norton.'

'Ah,' breathed Max, his interest rising. 'Is he the one with a wife on the way?'

'No. The Andrews are officially separated. They're Catholics; don't agree with divorce.'

'Mmm, got a football team of kids, I suppose.'

'Four, sir. They and their mother are back in Ireland.'

'Handy! Nothing to stop him fathering more children with other women. I'd say he's a strong candidate for this assault charge. Are Babs and Jerry still at the clinic?'

George nodded. 'It's a small place used by the wealthy. They're not too happy about British soldiers using their luxury rooms.' He added dryly, 'They'd probably tolerate officers more easily. Their main concern seems to be who's going to foot the bill.'

'They're copying the American practice of refusing to treat a casualty unless they have iron-clad proof of payment?'

'Oh no, sir, our guys are getting the best attention. I guess the clerical staff are faced with a situation they're unfamiliar with and are panicking somewhat over the finances.'

Max scowled. 'Anyone arriving at a hospital in the UK is treated for free, regardless of nationality, creed or condition. Are we a supremely humane nation, or dozy pushovers?'

'I think I'll pass on that one,' replied George, then addressed the subject most concerning him. 'You'll want to question Staff Andrews about his link with Norton, so can I hand the three casualties over to SIB? Tom and I were discussing that when you arrived. We've done the ground work, and if you're going to chase the relevance of that photograph . . .'

'It won't mean we're relieving you of the RTA,' Max intervened firmly.

'That's what I told him,' said Tom.

George was tenacious. 'Look, sir, the West Wilts are returning from Afghanistan tomorrow. You know what it's like when guys have been on active service and haven't had a beer for six months. Or a woman. The married ones are OK. It's the single guys who descend on the town and cause trouble. I've Styles on sick leave, and Morecombe in the UK on his bloody *honeymoon*. What does he want with that nonsense when he's been shagging Moira for the past three years? So I'm short-staffed just when some top brass are arriving for a high-powered conference.'

'Oh? When?'

'Day after tomorrow. Far as we know they're coming to parley with the West Wilts commanders on the up-to-date situation out there.' He pulled a wry face. 'Safer to do it here than wearing a flak jacket in a war zone. They still need guarding, of course, which'll leave me short of men for patrols down town.'

Max understood the problem. The six-monthly changeover of deployed troops was always a hectic time, and this would be the first since the arrival of the Scottish Drumdorran Fusiliers, whose addition had the base practically splitting at the seams. The uniformed squad had consequently been augmented by just two corporals, in accordance with the latest defence cuts. SIB's strength had stayed the same, which was another reason for clearing Piercey of the assault charge as soon as possible. And for himself to resume command, thought Max.

He turned to Tom. 'As we need to question Staff Andrews in connection with the Norton case, I suggest we keep tabs on all three at that clinic. Until they bring Andrews from the induced coma, we should send Connie to see what she can get from the one who's lucid enough to be questioned. She's an expert at coaxing men to confess all.'

A long moment passed before Tom asked, 'Are we talking official or just doing a favour?'

'In detectivespeak it's known as furthering our inquiries. At the end of the week George can have 'em back.' Max smiled at the immaculately uniformed sergeant. 'Call in your two. We'll send Connie Bush as soon as she reports in.'

George smiled back. 'Right, sir.'

'Email all data across to our headquarters. We'll take it from there.'

Once outside the Police Post Max challenged Tom. 'You're not happy with this?'

'It's not our territory.'

'I know, but we're straying into it because of the photograph of a woman who's laid false charges against one of ours . . . and because George has a lot on his plate with too few to handle it. I'm sure Connie will glean useful info for the Norton case.' He began walking to his car. 'Let's read the emails and chew it over some more with a mug of coffee in our hands.'

Tom caught up with him, demanding to know if he was officially resuming command.

Max faced his friend squarely. 'I can't sit around twiddling my thumbs for the next two weeks waiting to be told I'm fit to return to duty. I know I am. That photograph has put a new slant on the case; given us something to work on. I have a gut feeling there's a lot more to discover about Maria Norton, alias Carmen. I can't wait to begin removing the layers to reveal the real woman.'

'Has Captain Goodey given you the go ahead?' As Max

hesitated, Tom said, 'You'll be for the high jump when our revered Regional Commander hears what you're doing.'

'Let's hope he doesn't.' Max knew very well the basis of Tom's concern. 'Look, you're officially in command, and paid as such, until I'm medically cleared and reinstated. I'm merely showing an interest in the outcome of something affecting a member of the team I shall resume responsibility for in a fortnight's time. That's understandable enough, even for Keith Pinkney, surely.'

Partially reassured, Tom gave a faint grin. 'If he turns up I'll claim you pulled rank and ignored my protests.'

Max smiled back. 'He'll definitely understand that.'

Although it was still early, everyone was present busily engaged in writing up reports when they entered. Once coffee mugs had been filled, Tom began the briefing.

'Connie, you're to take over a task from Babs Turvey. Three of our personnel were involved in that massive RTA last night. They're at a private clinic in the vicinity of Grünwald, and one has in his wallet a photo of himself and Maria Norton in a romantic pose. We need background on that once the medics allow him to be questioned. George Maddox is emailing details across to us so, soon as we've heard your report, read them up and get over to the clinic. Staff Sergeant Andrews knows a lot we're anxious to share with him.'

'Right, sir,' said Connie, her usual sparklingly healthy appearance enhanced by a whirlwind romance with a bomb disposal sergeant encountered during their last case; a man whose commander blew himself and Max up last November.

'His injuries aren't life-threatening,' Tom continued, 'but he's being kept sedated to counteract trauma. You know the form. Work your magic on that man at the first opportunity. Now, give us your info on the search of Norton's car.'

'Nothing useful, I'm afraid. The guys in the car pool stripped it down with the utmost zeal, but only found the usual stuff that's in a vehicle used as a convenience, not a prized possession. Old parking tickets, chocolate wrappers, shopping lists between the cushions. The glove compartment held the operating manual, a small torch, a bag of cosmetics, another containing a spare pair of knickers and several tampons, a handbag aerosol of Hot Passion perfume and an opened pack of condoms.' She glanced up from her list. 'There was also an empty box for a CD of *Carmen*. The disc was not in the player. I checked Norton's room. It wasn't there, either.'

'Played to destruction,' said Tom dryly.

Connie had more. 'Phil called me with the info given by the taxi driver who had picked her up just short of the auto-bahn, so I followed up on it.'

She turned to Piercey, allowing him to offer the results of his search. He had dark shadows beneath eyes still dulled by the impact of what a woman he had chased after had done to him.

'Norton called Kwikcab at oh nine twenty-five asking to be met right away on the feeder road outside the base. She was lucky. They had a driver returning from an emergency dash to a maternity home, whose route would take him past the pick-up point within minutes. He reported that he expected to be sent to the hospital, because the young woman looked as if she had been in a car accident, although the vehicle she left beside the road seemed undamaged. He asked if she needed a doctor, but she ignored that and told him to get going in a manner he thought very rude. En route to the Imperial Hotel he noticed that she was crying, so he reversed his decision to make her take her own luggage out on arrival and he even carried it into the vestibule for her.'

Piercey gave a strained smile. 'He told me he had another change of heart when she failed to give him a tip. He departed in a temper and lost interest in her. He couldn't say whether anyone was waiting for her, or if she even checked in at the reception desk.'

Connie took up the narrative again. 'I made enquiries at the Imperial. They, of course, remembered a badly bruised young woman who refused their help, claiming she was waiting for her husband. She sat on their elegant settee for two hours looking upset and on the verge of collapse. The Concierge eventually called the hotel's nurse, not least because guests were demanding that something be done for her. Norton refused to go with the nurse and instead left the premises with her two bags.

'I spoke to the doorman. He had offered to call her a taxi, but she ignored him and walked to a nearby café. He doesn't recall seeing her come out from there, but he said she was swaying as she walked with what were probably heavy bags.'

Max was intrigued by all this, not having seen Maria Norton excelling on stage and later having been beaten up. 'What did the café staff have to say?' he asked, knowing Connie would have interviewed them.

'Well, sir, the Poppin Eaterie – the owners clearly watch a lot of American TV – is a very far cry from the Imperial, so a bruised and battered young woman didn't attract as much attention. She bought a mug of coffee and a meat sandwich.' She made a face. 'It's the kind of eaterie where meat is just meat. You don't get told which animal has provided it. That's the level of service they offer. However, the waitress remembered Norton using the pay phone three times, which surely suggests she no longer had her mobile.'

Closing her notebook, Connie slipped it into her pocket. 'There were only three staff. The waitress, a young girl making endless sandwiches and filled rolls, and a sour-faced man cooking frankfurters and other basic hot snacks. None of them could tell me when Norton left. Too busy, they said. So the trail goes cold there.'

'No, it doesn't,' Piercey disputed. 'A place like that would have regulars coming in at the same time each day for a lunch snack. One of them would surely have noticed a distressed girl using the payphone so often; would be able to tell us when she left and if she was alone or with someone. I could check that out.'

'You're too close to it,' ruled Tom immediately. 'Any part you play will be on this base.'

With a spurt of the old Piercey defiance, he said, 'Let

Derek do it, then. The sooner the better, while the memory's fresh.'

Beeny instantly volunteered to go there later that day. 'Norton summoned the taxi at oh nine twenty-five. Half an hour to reach the Imperial, two hours in the foyer, that means she'd be at the Poppin Eaterie during the very period when workers do drop in to grab a sandwich or roll. A bruised and battered girl swaying on her feet and carrying her belongings in two travel bags, how many of them do you see at your lunch place?'

'Yes OK!' snapped Tom. 'Go during *your* lunch break.'

Max attempted to calm things. 'It's certain Norton expected to meet someone at the Imperial. When he failed to turn up, she called him from the café. We do need to know if she left there with a companion. We'd meet with the usual blank wall if we tried to trace the number she called through the phone company, and it's too much to hope a customer noticed which digits she kept punching out. Is there any news on Norton's mobile yet?'

'I checked with the orderly at the Medical Centre, and with Babs Turvey. Zilch! I'd guess it's lying somewhere near the site of the attack,' said Piercey, then admitted that he had wandered last night over a large area surrounding the Recreation Centre punching in her number on his own mobile in the hope of hearing a ringing in response.

Heather Johnson put a damper on that. 'We've decided the assault took place near the RMP Post, so that was a waste of effort.'

Olly Simpson, busily doodling, murmured, 'It'll need recharging by now. Wherever it is it won't ring. Basic common knowledge.'

'For God's sake let's have more of that, and less Poirot-esque racking of little grey cells,' Tom ruled, as Connie moved across to her computer to access the emails coming in from George Maddox.

Heather had not finished. 'I went to HQ's QM Stores and asked Private James several plain questions. Could he identify who was driving Phil's Audi when it was backed out from where he had seen it parked ten minutes earlier? No. Not even a glimpse? No. Could he swear it was Phil who put it there? No, but he would swear the bloke was the same height and build, although he was wearing some kind of fancy dress.' She glanced up from her notes. I'd say that was a good enough identification. How many Spanish picadors live in the Sergeants' Mess?'

'There's no proof the guy James saw lived in the Mess. He came out again ten minutes later,' Olly pointed out in another murmur.

'He can't swear it was the same man,' Heather said heatedly.

'He can't swear either of the men he saw was Phil.'

'That guy's useless as a witness,' Piercey told them. 'He only sees tailors' dummies. He never looks at faces. If you speak to him you can see he's mentally measuring you up for a suit.'

'But he recognizes *cars*,' Heather countered, 'and he's prepared to swear it was yours that arrived when you claim you did.' She then produced her rabbit from a hat. 'He's also prepared to swear he saw another car parked outside the gymnasium when he took his walk after the late night film. At first he believed a couple were having a snog, but it was empty which he thought was an odd place to park for the night.'

'Did he get the reg number?' Tom asked eagerly.

'Unfortunately, no, nor could he tell me the make. But he was certain it was red.'

Olly Simpson looked up in astonishment. 'There's a man on this base who can't identify the make of a car?'

'He was mentally measuring it for a suit,' muttered Piercey.

Seeing Tom's mounting irritation, Max intervened. 'Even anonymous cars have drivers, which means there was someone in close proximity who could have seen Phil return and decided to borrow his Audi as cover for some business he was loath to use his own wheels for. It's a start.' He nodded at Piercey. 'Job for you. Trace all owners of red vehicles. Any of them who haven't an alibi for the early hours of Sunday morning can be investigated further.'

From her desk at the rear of the Incident Room, Connie called out, 'Norton's Clio is red.'

'So Norton swapped her vehicle for Phil's before meeting the man who attacked her, then Chummy returned it to pick up hers to leave outside her quarters where we found it on Sunday morning?' suggested Heather.

'Why would she do that?' demanded Beeny.

'How else did her car return to her accommodation block? We haven't considered that yet,' she responded rounding on him.

'She could have been attacked there when she left the vehicle.'

'Then she would have gone to her room instead of crawling halfway across the base to the RMP Post.'

Max intervened. 'Instead of wasting time on speculation, better to show Private James the Clio and ask if its shape is like the one he saw parked outside the gymnasium.'

Tom agreed, and embarked on the results of his interview with Bill Jensen. 'As we've already pretty well decided, Norton's story was pure invention. Bill confirmed that she'd said she needed to make a phone call before leaving the theatre.' He glared at the amorous sergeant. 'Possibly to the person she was speaking to when you interrupted her in her dressing room. The melodrama that followed delayed it, but Jensen said she waffled on about it being important. He didn't see her with the phone, and when he went backstage to check on her she'd obviously left through the stage door which was swinging open. We need to find that mobile.'

'If we knew where she was attacked there'd be a better chance of tracing it,' grumbled Beeny.

'I'm now going to broaden the canvas even further. Jensen told me when he began to chivvy the loiterers to leave, Norton was up on the stage drinking red wine with three admirers who she then kissed and shooed down the steps to the auditorium. I want to know who they were and where they went on leaving. Then there's the wild card. On the same nights as rehearsals for *Carmen* classes in woodwork, photography, higher mathmatics, music and movement, German and Spanish were held. Chummy might have attended one and become hooked on Norton in her role as Carmen – particularly if he was studying Spanish.' He gave Piercey another unfriendly glare. 'When we run out of possibles we'll have to check attendees of all those classes.'

'Not music and movement,' murmured Heather. 'The title alone would scare men off.'

Max smiled. 'Probably. It seems to me there's a cluster of likely suspects still to be investigated. Plenty to be getting on with, so I'll help out where I can.'

Ten minutes later the room was empty apart from himself, Tom and Piercey who was condemned to the task of tracing all car owners and isolating those whose vehicles were red. Max invited Tom to his office for privacy and when they were seated said finding Maria Norton was the priority.

'She's a member of the personnel on this base, which makes her our responsibility. She's also a pregnant young woman who's been beaten up on our patch and, from what we know of her behaviour after leaving here, she's in a distressed state trying to link up with someone she believes will help her. We need to contact her parents, particularly the mother she claims called to ask how the final performance went down. She's probably the most likely port in a storm for her daughter.'

'She's Spanish. Explains why Norton was so believable as Carmen. That's only common knowledge because of the general interest in the show. Nothing's been circulated about the father. I'll check him out.'

As if he sensed a hint of criticism, he frowned. 'She only went off twenty-four hours ago. I had Piercey set up the usual alerts and, as you just heard, he traced the taxi driver who picked her up. Alongside that we've been investigating a serious assault of which a member of our staff has been wrongly accused and appears to have been deliberately set up. In my book, that's a greater crime than a woman who's excused duty on medical grounds deciding to take herself off without permission.'

'Lower those hackles, Tom, I'd have acted the same way,' said Max frankly. I'm simply making observations on what I heard. We appear to have two cases: what's behind Norton's behaviour and who's mounting a campaign against Piercey.'

'But they're linked, because she's adamant it was he who attacked her.'

Max nodded. 'Of course they're linked. Solve one, solve the other. Yet I sense a complexity which will probably hamper us whichever direction we take.' He stretched to ease an ache starting between his shoulder blades. 'We'll know more by the end of today. One aspect I find intriguing. Norton is apparently a talented singer, yet her military career appears to be thriving. Could that be because the father of her child is a squadron colleague?'

'It's possible. I reckon the Doc's nutshell theory is still the most likely. Norton broke the news and refused to have an abortion; he lashed out with his fists. If it wasn't the father who attacked her why hasn't the bastard been comforting her and raging about what he'll do to the bugger when he gets hold of him? Doesn't add up, does it?'

'If he's a civilian he might not know she's been assaulted. Maybe she was trying to tell him on the phone in the eaterie.'

'But she gave every sign of expecting someone to be waiting for her at the Imperial.'

'And when he didn't turn up after two hours she tried to call him from the greasy spoon place, where she wouldn't be overheard.'

As they both considered that they heard Piercey's voice followed by a lighter, feminine one. Then a tap fell on the door. The visitor brought both men wordlessly to their feet, gazing at a slim woman in her early twenties whose perfect features, black hair and dark almond eyes betrayed the Oriental blood in her genealogy. She was far too beautiful to be clad in warriors' garb.

'Captain Rydal?' she queried, looking from one to the other of the two men in similar dark suits.

'Yes, and Sergeant Major Black, my second in command,' Max said indicating Tom. 'How can we help you?'

'I'm not sure. It's difficult to know just what to do.'

Max smiled. 'You don't strike me as a person who can't handle a problem swiftly and professionally. You wouldn't be in the job you have otherwise.' Noting her Signals badge and lieutenant's rank, he added, 'You've come to talk about Corporal Norton?'

'Yes. I'm Su Carfax, B Troop Commander.'

'So sit down and tell us why you're here. Mr Black is the best person to consult. I'm merely sitting in during the last few days of my convalescent leave. He knows the details better than I.'

Tom rose to that. 'Have you some info for us, ma'am? Has Norton made contact with you?'

'No, nothing like that,' she murmured, settling on one of the chairs facing the desk.

'I shall be sending members of my team to question Norton's colleagues, and the senior NCOs too. This would have been done as part of our investigation on the assault made on her, but her decision to cut and run has put the emphasis on discovering why. Whether she ran *from* or *to* someone. The fact that she's two months pregnant adds complications. She refused to tell me the name of the father.'

She frowned. 'I was unaware of that until I visited the Medical Centre on returning from weekend leave. She was sleeping.'

'How well do you know Maria Norton?' asked Max, unable to stay aloof.

'As well as she allows anyone to know her,' came the thoughtful reply. 'She has two enthusiasms. Her work and her singing.'

'Shouldn't that be three?' asked Tom pointedly. 'From our questioning so far we've learned she's also very enthusiastic about men.'

A flicker of annoyance touched those almost black eyes. 'As are a large number of women on this base. Norton is in line for promotion, but her actions will negate that. It's a great pity. She must have taken that into account before making the decision to endanger her career.'

'Surely the decision was taken after the assault, which she would not have been expecting,' Max pointed out. 'On the slim evidence we have so far, I'd say she ran to avoid further punishment from her assailant. Do you know something that points to a different conclusion?'

The young subaltern hesitated. 'Corporal Norton is one of a team handling highly classified information.'

'And?' Max prompted.

'I agreed to her request to work the day shift from eight to seventeen hundred during the four performances of the opera, which doesn't mean she had no leeway over taking her normal break periods.'

'Yes?' said Tom impatiently.

Another short hesitation. 'At noon on Saturday a particularly sensitive item came through, which Norton authenticated.'

'Concerning someone on this base?'

'I can't tell you that, Mr Black.'

'But you think it's behind Norton's decision to run?' When she said nothing, Max probed further. 'It could have prompted the assault on her?'

'I've come here to ask what you've uncovered about this sorry affair in the hope of being reassured.'

'That's unlikely. You've just added a further complication.' Then Max asked sharply, 'This classified information; does it concern a member of my team?'

'Sergeant Piercey? No. You asked because he's under investigation for the attack on Norton?'

'No longer. We've proved Norton's account of what happened is completely unsubstantiated. My sergeant has been set up, presumably by the real perpetrator.'

'Or by Norton herself,' put in Tom. 'I'll tell you what we know as of now and maybe you can add to our perception of her.'

At the end of Tom's concise precis, Su Carfax denied any

knowledge of her corporal's involvement with Staff Sergeant Andrews.

'I deal with their professional problems, that's all. I'm not their nanny. Their private lives are private. Unless they approach me for advice I respect their right to occupy their off duty time as they wish.'

'Providing it's within the law,' said Tom.

Again there was a flicker of annoyance in her eyes. 'Maria Norton is a very attractive woman, and knows it, but she's very intelligent, enthusiastic and first class at her job. I can only believe she was under immense pressure for her to do what she has. She had everything going for her. Certain promotion, widespread applause for her portrayal of Carmen, an offer to sing with the Drumdorran band when they give concerts. These things would be immensely important to her. As I said before, her military career and her singing are her great enthusiasms. She spends as much as her colleagues spend on clothes to pay for lessons with a coach in town. And because her neighbours complained, she persuaded one of the PT Instructors to allow her to use an office in the gymnasium for her vocal exercises. That's how keen she is.'

Max said with a smile, 'I think you undersold yourself just now. You do take an interest in the off duty pursuits of your troop members.'

'It's impossible not to with someone as vivid as she.'

Tom broke into the duologue.' Do you know the name of the singing teacher?'

'I'm sorry. Is it important?'

'Could be, if she's holed-up with him right now.'

There was a quiet moment before Lieutenant Carfax stood, setting the men also on their feet. 'So we have reached no conclusion on why Corporal Norton left the base in a painful and bruised state, risking those things that are so important to her.'

'Nor do we yet know why she made a damaging false accusation against our sergeant,' Tom replied bluntly. 'That'll be added to any further charges she might incur.'

Max walked towards the door with the visitor. 'Are you at all reassured on the problem you came here with?'

'No, that will only come when you unearth the truth. Or when . . .' She broke off and hurried to the main entrance with mumbled thanks.

As Max stood watching her, Tom came up beside him. 'Well, well, what was that all about?'

'Yes. Interesting. Norton apparently saw something damning about a person on this base, and they're afraid she informed him, got a beating to make her keep quiet and ran to get away from him.'

The more prosaic Tom said, 'They only have to interrogate him.'

'But they'd risk betraying classified info if their theory is wrong. All the same, whatever they know must be high octane stuff to cause such concern.'

FIVE

Returning to Max's office to consider this new development in relation to what they already knew about the case, they had not progressed far when Piercey appeared in the doorway.

'The Regional Commander has just driven up, sir.'

Max pulled a face. 'Oh God! Tom, this is where you tell him I pulled rank on you.'

'Why would you have done that? You've simply called in in passing, hoping for coffee and a bun.'

'So I have,' he replied with a grin as Piercey returned to his desk.

Tall and thin, with a neat brown moustache, Major Keith Pinkney was known to regret his appointment to senior office. A man of action, he now saw himself as no more than a meddler in other men's investigations when he yearned to run his own once more. With the appointment came the abundance of paperwork to tie him to his desk – an occupation he considered only the most complete philistine would relish.

Walking directly to where Max and Tom were now standing casually alongside the shelf bearing an electric kettle and a selection of mugs, Pinkney's strident voice accused Max.

'Heard you were back and putting your spoke in where it shouldn't be, Captain Rydal.'

Straightening to attention beside Tom, Max said genially, while cursing the fact that there were spies on the base, 'Good morning, sir. Can we offer you some coffee?'

'Certainly can,' came the clipped reply. 'And while I'm drinking it you can explain how you came to so badly miscalculate the length of your convalescent leave.'

Setting about making coffee, Tom said diplomatically, 'I'll bring it to Captain Rydal's office when it's ready, sir.'

'Yes, do that, Mr Black. Don't go off anywhere. I shall want to hear of your progress on this tacky business that's under way.'

Back in his office Max knew subterfuge was useless. Who the hell had ratted on him? Pinkney remained standing, for which Max was glad. The ache between his shoulders was increasing and being upright allowed him to ease it by movement.

'You know you're due to face a medical board next month, Max. D'you want to pass it and get back to work, or take chances which could delay that for another month? Or two?' Into the pause, he asked, 'Have you even had a check-up with the MO?'

Max ignored that last. 'I flew in from Spain on Sunday night to learn that Sergeant Piercey, one of my own team, had been accused of violent assault against a female corporal. I not unnaturally wanted the details, feeling certain it was a case of mistaken identity because the scenario didn't fit what I know of Piercey. All I have done is talk to him man to man to assess his defence. That was yesterday. When I heard the girl had gone AWOL I decided to come in this morning for the briefing, which I hoped would go some way to supporting Piercey's assertion that he's innocent of the charge.' He looked Pinkney in the eye to add, 'I've not "put my spoke in" anything. Tom Black is still commanding the Section, and making a fine job of it, sir. As for the Doc, she was on the spot in the company of Major MacPherson when that tanker hit a load of gas cylinders last night, so they spent the greater part of it helping with the casualties. There's been no opportunity for me to get checked out by either of them . . . yet.'

Tom had clearly been eavesdropping, for he made a nicely timed entrance with the coffee. Pinkney took the bone china mug reserved for visiting seniors, then sank on one of the chairs facing Max's desk.

'Sit down, both of you. Fill me in on where you've got to on this assault case.'

Although Max took his usual chair behind his desk, he made

no attempt to lead the conversation. Tom gave a precis of the stage they had reached in what appeared to be two cases tenuously linked to Phil Piercey.

'He's dumbfounded, sir. Has no idea why he's being victimized, or by whom.'

'It's more than likely to be someone whom Piercey crossed during a past case. An eye for an eye.'

'Or he just happens to be a handy scapegoat,' offered Max. 'Norton must have known her fiction would be easily disproved. My guess is that, in her state of collapse after the beating, his name was the obvious one to quote in order to avert blame from someone she tried to shield, or was afraid to betray.' Warming to his theme, he added, 'There's obviously a deeper issue here. Why else would Norton run?'

Pinkney eyed him speculatively. 'Haven't put your spoke in? Balls! Captain Goodey knew what she was doing when she installed you far away in Spain. Only way to make you relax and heal, man.'

'I *have* healed. I'm back to full fitness . . . as she'll be forced to record when I finally manage to secure an appointment for a check-up.'

The Regional Commander stood, causing the other two to do the same. 'Thank you for bringing me up to speed with this rather disturbing affair, Tom. Early days, yet, but keep me informed on a daily basis. We'll do our best to keep it out of the tabloids, but there's always a blabbermouth willing to tell tales.'

'*Isn't* there, sir,' agreed Max pointedly.

Pinkney laughed. 'Keep a low profile for the next two weeks. Nourishing food, nothing too strenuous, and early nights. Maybe a little light reading such as a detective story concerning an SIB sergeant wrongly accused of ABH.' He offered his hand. 'Good to see you back on your feet, Max, and with everything intact. Any problems, call me.'

Turning to Tom, he said, 'You've done a first class job over the past four months. Don't let him rob you of the last few days.'

*   *   *

Returning to the subject of Su Carfax's concern over an item of sensitive information Maria Norton had been made aware of, Max and Tom hammered out the possible influence it might have had on the pregnant woman's subsequent actions.

Tom delivered the coup de grace to the Signals' lieutenant's fears. 'I watched Norton give a bravura performance on stage only eight hours after receiving that transmission, and another of equal vivacity at the party that followed. Bill Jensen saw her still flirting with three admirers when he was waiting to lock the place up. Is that the behaviour of a woman worried by what she had been privy to?'

'A red herring?' suggested Max.

'One we should put in the freezer and only defrost when all else has been chewed over and spat out.'

'Or when . . . as the Anglo-Chinese beauty left tantalizingly unfinished.' Max frowned. 'I suspect there's another storm brewing which, when it arrives, could very probably concern SIB.'

Any comment Tom might have made on that was deferred by the ring tone of Max's mobile. His expression as he answered sent Tom hotfoot from the room.

'Good morning, Captain Goodey,' Max said, knowing Keith Pinkney had meant what he said.

'Where are you?'

'About ten minutes' drive from where you are.'

'I'll look for you in ten minutes, then.'

'Yes, ma'am.'

He hummed lightheartedly as he travelled the perimeter road. Just the sound of Clare's voice had banished the ache between his shoulders. Also the feeling that he was on the outside looking in. As he approached the Medical Centre he saw Clare emerge and stand waiting. Their reunion would have been better at the riverside inn, but the sight of her put such warmth in his veins he had no further doubts about the kind of relationship he wanted with this calm but commanding woman. He recalled her words at their intitial meeting. 'I'm small, slim and female, but don't let any man on this base underestimate me.'

He drew up and was surprised when she slid on to the passenger seat. 'Follow that car,' she instructed in the manner of film detectives, pointing to a three-ton truck lumbering past.

'With siren and flashing blue lights?' he asked teasingly.

She kept her eyes on the road. 'There'll be sirens and flashing lights by the time I've finished with you. Park your car in the empty slot furthest from the Mess, unless you want everyone to hear what I'm going to say, then fall silent when we enter.'

Only then did he realize that she was seriously angry, and swiftly prepared a defence. Reaching the Officers' Mess, he drove to the far side of the car park where the hedge that had been burned down four months ago showed signs of springtime new growth. Coming to a halt with the bonnet facing away from the large square building he switched off, released the seat belt and turned to face her.

'What the hell do you think you're doing?' she demanded with quiet venom, her blue eyes blazing. 'You'd already gone when I woke up this morning; gone without leaving a message for me. I assumed you'd headed for the nearest supermarket to stock up, then Duncan came in just now and mentioned that he'd seen you going into SIB Headquarters a couple of hours ago.'

Trust him to be the one who reported my movements to her, Max thought savagely, jealousy of the large, handsome Scot still lurking beneath the surface of his feelings for Clare.

'The three months' leave considered necessary for convalescence by a panel of doctors when you left the hospital has two more weeks to run. You then have to undergo a thorough examination by that same panel before any decision is made on your fitness to return to full duties.'

'I haven't,' he protested, but she was not listening.

'You left Spain without reference to me, and . . .'

'I ensured your property was spotless and secure.'

'. . . and sneaked into your apartment hoping I wouldn't know you were back, but you forgot my Sunday ritual of inspecting your apartment. I had to learn of your covert return by being scared out of my wits on seeing a body in your bed.'

'It wasn't a covert return,' he began, remembering guiltily how he had ensured no lights would be seen at the front of the building. 'You weren't there when I arrived, and I was tired after the flight.'

'There are pens and paper, emails, mobile phones. No, you sneaked in expressly to avoid me.'

'*You weren't there*,' he repeated emphatically.

'Had you told me you were coming home I would have been.'

'I wanted to surprise you,' he wheedled with sudden inspiration.

'Don't try to avoid the issue using blatant cajolery that's so out of character it's laughable.'

'I've forgotten what the issue is, ma'am.'

'No, you haven't,' she snapped. 'Now you're back on the base you've become one of my patients again, and I refuse to allow you to undertake any form of military duty until passed by a medical board. You sustained serious injuries in that explosion. A foot closer and you'd have been killed along with Jeremy Knott. I thought you had more sense than the average male who thinks it's macho to defy medical advice, then ends up twice as ill.'

'Clare, I'm not being irresponsibly stupid.' He tried to take her hand, but she pushed his away. 'I hear what you're saying, but you know damn well there are hundreds of instances when doctors are proved wrong. Miracles of mind over matter, or a guardian angel hovering. I know my body took a beating in that explosion. It ached, it burned, it produced so much pain I thought it would never end. But it has. A week ago I suddenly realized I was back to normal.

'No, don't look at me that way,' he chided. 'Consider your car, for instance. You jump in it and take for granted that it will get you safely to your destination. *But*, if you hear a faint rattle or squeak; hesitation when the engine fires; smell burning or petrol; feel the vehicle juddering or losing power up hills you know there's something wrong.

'Being inside your skin is similar to that. Day after day you take for granted that your body is doing what it should. *But*, a slight twinge; a curious ache or pain; trembling or giddiness; losing power up hills all tell you that something's wrong. A week ago I knew this large bulk of flesh, bones and organs named Rydal was working completely normally again. It still is. So much so, the brain that goes with it needs similar stimulation after three months of books, music, jigsaw puzzles and Mollie Hubbard.'

He managed to catch up her hand this time. 'I appreciate your care and concern, all you've done for me over the bad four months, but I've come through it and I'm ready to take up my life where it left off last November.' He squeezed her fingers. 'I'm not a fighting soldier intending to go to a warzone any day now, I'm just helping to investigate a false charge against one of my men. Some in-depth thinking isn't going to threaten my chances at the medical board.'

She studied him for several moments without drawing her hand away. 'Have you finished?'

'Yes. Can we kiss and make up?'

'In front of the Officers' Mess?' she cried in mock horror. 'That'll have to wait until tonight. Come on, let's go in for lunch and you can tell me about your thrilling escape from Mother Hubbard.'

When Max left Headquarters Tom shut himself in his own office leaving Piercey sitting gloomily before his computer. On checking out Maria Norton's next of kin he was surprised. Although he ought not to have been because the young singer was intelligent enough to hold NCO rank in a specialized branch of the Army.

That her mother was Spanish was generally known due to gossip over *Carmen*, but Tom was sure few people on the base were aware that Maria Norton was the daughter of a professor of advanced mathematics at a redbrick university in the UK. Alusha Norton was at an address in New York, which suggested a divorce or legal separation. Tom doubted Maria had planned to join her father, or to cross the Atlantic, so he sought more productive action by calling Bill Jensen. When the former sergeant major picked up, Tom could hear small children singing discordantly in the background.

He laughed. 'Is that the next Orpheus Choir rehearsing, Bill?'

'It's the pre-school kiddies being calmed down before their mums come to collect them. Singing works wonders. So, I heard Milady Norton has hopped it. Silly bitch! Why do so many women screw up their lives? She had a successful career under way, and a hobby she excelled at. I was yarning to the Drumdorran's Bandmaster yesterday – he conducted the orchestra for *Carmen* – and he's mad keen for her to do some concerts with them; even go out to Afghanistan to sing for the lads. Sort of posh Forces' Sweetheart. Great opportunity for her, but I'm not sure it would be wise to let her loose among sex-starved soldiers. Would they be safe?' He followed that with a gusty laugh.

Tom's heart sank. They had forgotten about the musicians. Another thirty susceptible men who had watched Norton's tantalizing performance on stage every night for a week.

'You sing with a choir, Bill. Know a lot of locals who're into music and singing. Norton apparently had lessons with a vocal coach. Can you offer any names, suggest who might have been teaching her?'

Jensen sucked his teeth noisily. 'Ooh, there you've got me. There's a couple of baritones in my choir who give lessons, but I guess they'd be pretty basic. Same as those listed in the phone book. Nowhere good enough for a voice like hers. The more top notch guys don't need to promote themselves.'

'Well, thanks anyway.'

'Hang on, Tom. I'll give Gisela a call. She'll know a lot more about classical musicians living locally. Her province is ballet, but she grew up in the music world and will surely know all the local maestros. Get back to you.'

A glance at the clock gave Tom two options: take an early lunch or visit the Drumdorran Fusiliers' Bandmaster. Mmm, perhaps get that interview over before tackling a meal.

Captain Rory Staines had an office at the front of the block housing practice rooms, a large performance hall and living quarters for whichever regimental band happened to be stationed on the base. This was the first time since Tom arrived in Germany that bagpipes were predominant . . . and he loathed bagpipes.

Although each practice room was reasonably sound-proofed, it was possible for anyone walking the corridor to hear muffled versions of what was being rehearsed in each of them, and Tom's ears protested at what seemed like the sounds of purgatory. He swiftly knocked on the Bandmaster's door and was glad to be invited to enter.

Captain Staines was around Tom's age, with much the same colouring but slighter of build. He was also very much the gentleman, speaking with received pronunciation and displaying the natural assurance of men who have been raised knowing their elevated place in society. He smiled and waited to be appraised of the identity of this large man wearing a dark suit with what could be a regimental tie.

'Sarn't Major Black, SIB, sir,' he said crisply. 'Could you spare a few minutes to help with my enquiries into the violent assault on Corporal Maria Norton in the early hours of Sunday morning?'

A flash of something Tom interpreted as unease crossed the man's face before he said, 'A deplorable business. I heard she's been hospitalized.'

'Yes, sir.' He decided not to qualify that belief at this stage.

'I'm unable to think of any way I can be of help, Mr Black. I know nothing about the young woman. Apart from the musical connection, of course.'

'You must have spent quite some time with her during rehearsals; gained some impression of her personality as divorced from her stage role.'

The light laugh was forced. 'It's plain you've had no experience of operatic performance.'

Staines made no attempt to continue, and the fact that Tom had been kept standing in front of the man's desk like a supplicating squaddie told Tom he had touched on a sensitive spot. He persevered.

'I did attend the final performance of *Carmen*. My wife made a number of costumes for the chorus.'

'Ah.'

At this second attempt to end the interview Tom grew more determined. 'I'm afraid the case has become more serious. We believe Corporal Norton may be involved in something likely to result in further attacks on her. We're questioning everyone who was involved in the opera, both backstage and on it. With some urgency, sir. A serious crime was committed against Norton just minutes after she left the theatre, and the most likely perpetrator was someone connected with *Carmen*. My staff will need to speak to every one of your musicians, so . . .'

'Impossible!' Staines ejaculated swiftly. 'We're giving a concert in town on Thursday. Then we give a marching display and Beat the Retreat here on Friday to entertain the West Wiltshire troops arrived back from Afghanistan, while simultaneously putting on a show for a group of senior officers coming here for tactical discussions with them. My musicians will be working flat out for the rest of this week. After that . . .'

'Captain Staines,' Tom said, determinedly interrupting the senior man this time. 'It's not a question of being inconvenient. Every single person involved with that opera has to be considered a suspect until they provide proof that will eliminate them from the list. I appreciate that your schedule is tight, but your full cooperation will reduce the time we spend with your musicians.' He gave Staines time to absorb that, then said, 'Tell me what you know about Maria Norton, please.'

As if reluctant to invite Tom to sit, the officer got to his feet and crossed to gaze from the window which gave a view of the performance hall.

'She has an amazing voice. I had great reservations about the decision to stage *Carmen*. Any opera is difficult for amateurs to tackle. I wish they would stick to operetta;

much lighter stuff which suffers less from enthusiastic but untrained voices. When the principals came here for the initial try out I was . . . stunned.' That descriptive word was spoken more softly and reflectively. 'Don Jose and Escamillo had sufficient power to cope with the demands of their roles, and I knew they'd improve after weeks of rehearsal. But Maria! She *was* Carmen. Right from the start. She had the allure, the sexual promise, the teasing gestures, the *magnetism.*'

He turned to face Tom. 'That's all I know about her. I'm a musician, Sarn't Major. Apart from my dear wife and children, music is my whole life. Watching and hearing that young woman perform was one of those unexpected privileges that happen only so often. She's wasting her talent. I tried to persuade her she could use her voice and still remain in the Army. I was eager to arrange for her to sing with us at concerts, not just locally but when we tour, but it fell on deaf ears.' His eyes narrowed in reflection. 'She never emerged from her role. It was almost as if she had been taken over by Carmen,' he added with the same suggestion of unease Tom had detected earlier. 'That attack on her echoed the tragedy that ends the opera.'

Left alone in their headquarters, Piercey gloomily checked the lists of vehicles registered as being permitted to pass back and forth the base. He highlighted every red one regardless of make or shape. There were a small number of Clios, but none were red. Maria Norton was recorded as owning a cream one. The reg number he knew by heart, so she must have had it sprayed and failed to report the fact.

His hands dropped from the keyboard to his lap as misery swamped him yet again. How could he have made such a gallumping idiot of himself over her? All the time she had flirted and teased him she had known she was carrying some poor sap's child. Small wonder the bloke had lost it and slapped her around. Stood to reason no man would put up with sharing her with all and sundry.

But why frame *him* specifically? Had Maria lied to her lover about that incident in the dressing room; claimed he had tried to rape her? If that had been the case, surely any red-blooded bloke would do more than take a car and return it half an hour later by way of retaliation. He would more likely have lain in wait for the opportunity to beat him up, too.

Now Maria had put herself beyond questioning the bloody case would run on and on . . . and he would remain in a grey zone doing all the crap jobs. His one hope was that Max would get him off the hook soon. Tom Black would try to be impartial, but would not be able to put aside his personal dislike completely. Thank God the Regional Commander had not put the official kibosh on the Boss's participation.

He glanced at the big MoD clock on the wall. Almost midday. He would go for some lunch. Buy snacks in the NAAFI, take them to his room and watch the Grand Prix on TV. It might take his mind off Black Maria – his new name for her!

Armed with a pack of beef and pickle sandwiches, two pork pies, a large bag of onion crisps and several Wagon Wheels, Piercey went back to his car feeling lighter-spirited already. He was innocent of everything save briefly touching her breasts. He could not be court martialled for that . . . and the truth would out eventually.

Clipping on his seat belt, he then opened the CD storage compartment. Strident music as he drove would raise his spirits further. His reaching hand suddenly froze as he stared at the fancy pink mobile phone bearing the word CARMEN in glittery silver stickers, which lay among his CDs.

He sat gazing at it for long moments, the overwhelming excitement of her returning unbidden. How many times had he called her; how many intimate texts had he sent? Dear God, the words he had whispered to her just two hours before that final performance, in the confidence that she would be in his bed that night. Heard out of context they could blow away his defence.

With a heedless need to rid himself of the incriminating

object, he drove around the perimeter road until he drew up level with the copse where residents walked dogs, or had picnics and family games in the summer. Pulling on a latex glove he picked up the mobile, the glittering CARMEN twisting the knife. If he lobbed it far enough it was unlikely to be discovered for some time, by when the case should be closed.

Leaving his car he strode across to where one of the narrower paths cut through denser trees . . . and immediately came face to face with two women who smiled and said hallo. Lolloping back and forth and all around them were four or five young dogs eagerly exploring the leafy undergrowth. They passed noisily leaving Piercey cold with shock. He had intended to hide vital evidence!

Waiting long enough for the women to pack themselves and their animals in a Range Rover before driving away, he returned to his car and sat staring once more at that silver word that caught the sun. She had been acting a role on and off the stage. He had allowed himself to become obsessed with a fiction. That realization somehow made his humiliation worse.

As a wounded animal returns to its lair, he headed for the room which he had been allowed to reoccupy last night and tried to decide what to do. Maria had retained around thirty texts. Some of them would be his. If he deleted everything it would be as bad as hiding the bloody object in the copse, for there would also surely be messages from her attacker and the father of her baby. Feeling sick now, he charged the mobile up and waited.

With hands that were uncharacteristically unsteady he slowly brought up the texts one by one, his heartbeat thudding. Then he sat staring into space, fierce anger building until he snatched up the handset of his landline and punched in the number of Beeny's mobile.

'Where are you?' he asked when his friend answered.

'In town. At the Poppin Eaterie questioning the eaters. Problem?'

'I've just found Norton's mobile in the CD compartment of my Audi.'

'Ah! That *is* a problem. Chummy must have planted it there after beating her up.'

'There's worse, Derek. She's retained thirty texts. I've just read them expecting there'd be evidence of his identity; whoever made her pregnant.'

'And?'

'They're all texts I sent her. The bastard deleted the rest.'

After a short pause Beeny asked, 'Haven't you *any* idea of who's behind this?'

'No, I bloody haven't,' he practically yelled. 'I keep telling you that. If I had d'you think I'd be sitting here beating my brains out trying to decide what to do?'

'Do about what?'

'These texts. They're pretty steamy. Without input from other people it could suggest sexual harassment on my part. They were actually sent over a period of two months, and mostly in response to teasing messages from her . . . which I foolishly haven't retained.'

'Pity! Her mobile provider will be as adamant as the national telecom company about giving us info on calls made and received by her over the relevant period, so if Chummy's deleted everything your discovery doesn't get us any further forward.'

'That's what I thought,' he said. 'So these texts are of no importance.'

'Inasmuch as they're apparently cringe-making they'll prove how far from basic sanity you'd strayed where she was concerned.'

'I'm getting sick of hearing that,' he snapped. 'We have ample witness to the fact that the case against me is a non-starter, so . . .'

'So what?'

He rushed into it. 'So if these texts were deleted, like the rest, it wouldn't affect the investigation.'

'Christ, Phil!' A significant silence. 'I didn't hear that.'

His anger still burned brightly. 'Are you a friend or a policeman?' he demanded.

'A policeman *would* have heard it and start writing a report about evidence being tampered with by the accused.'

Piercey hit out. 'So you believe I beat her up!'

'No! But I do think you're treading on eggshells over this. So it'll be degrading to have your hot messages read by your colleagues, especially Heather, but I can work it so that just Olly and I deal with it and write the report.'

'Yeah, which can then be accessed by the rest of the team.'

'Grow up, Phil!'

That really stung, because he knew in his heart that he had behaved over Maria like a teenager suffering from juvenile infatuation. Snatching up the mobile he had placed in an evidence bag, he got to his feet.

'Thanks for your input, Sergeant Beeny. I'm taking the evidence to Headquarters immediately. Don't want anyone tampering with it.'

SIX

'I was at the show. I watched her for almost two hours and heard her sing. I attended the self-indulgent party that followed, and viewed her close up. Then I drove us all home and went happily to bed with you, enjoying young Christopher's antics against my hand on your stomach.'

'What's your point, Tom?' asked Nora, sitting on the sofa beside him with her head against his shoulder.

'I've spent two days listening to eulogies on Maria Norton aka Carmen. Blokes were prepared to fight over her, they clustered around her at that party as if attached by superglue. Ron Parkin, a walking Adonis, bends the rules to allow her to use the gym to practise her arias . . . and Christ knows what else! A staff sergeant with a wife and four kids in Ireland carries a photo in his wallet of himself in a clinch with her. She turned Phil Piercey from macho man to simpering mouse – you should read his text messages to her – and the Bandmaster has been "stunned" by an operatic fantasy. I swear he's waiting for news that she's been killed by a jealous lover to bring on a full artistic orgasm.'

She chuckled softly against his sleeve. 'And you're worried that you're losing your sexual drive because you get more satisfaction from feeling your son kicking my innards?'

'I telephoned the vocal coach she's been taking lessons from. Gisela Bensen knew who it was. Now, he's a retired bass who's actually been on stage with Domingo once or twice, so he must be a sophisticated performer of discerning age. He raved about her, practically broke down on hearing what's happened. Promised to look for her in the cafés and coffee houses they frequent for discussions after lessons. Dirty old devil!'

Nora laughed outright. 'You don't know that.'

'I can make an informed guess.'

'It's not informed, it's biased.' She sat straighter. 'Let's have a drink before the girls arrive like a ravenous horde. There's only three of them, but they fall on food like twice the number.'

'Wait until young Christopher develops his appetite. He'll give them a run for their money.' He got up and filled two large glasses with red wine. 'What's for supper?'

'Chicken casserole with dumplings, followed by apricot mousse.'

'Two of my favourites.' He settled beside her again and touched his glass to hers. '*Prost*! Nora, why would *I* lust after any other woman when I have you?' Next moment he grew surprisingly emotional. 'Without you I'd be nothing, you know that, don't you?'

She kissed him gently. 'Softie!'

They drank their wine in reflective silence until Nora returned to the subject of Maria Norton. 'There've been no reports of her whereabouts? No sightings?'

'Beeny went to the caff where she reportedly ate a sandwich and made three calls on the public phone. He stayed for an hour and a half, questioning those who came in for a lunch snack. The only success was a statement from a young Frenchman, who said he saw her leaving as he entered. Had to stand aside to allow her through with a couple of heavy bags. Beeny rated him a bit of a weirdo, but his description of Norton rang true. The witness thought she'd turned right, which would have taken her back past the Imperial, so Beeny asked there if she had returned. A snooty undermanager told him she had caused trouble and upset their guests, so the doorman had been told not to admit her if she should come back. The Imperial did not count common soldiers as desirable guests!'

'Poor girl,' said Nora with feeling. 'Imagine if it was one of ours in that predicament.'

'*She* made the decision to abscond,' Tom pointed out. 'Clare Goodey was looking after her medically, and we were quick off the mark with our investigation. I was called from my bed

at three in the morning and worked all day Sunday on it, if
you recall. The Army was doing its best for her.'

'I know, love, but from what you've told me she had no
friends on the base. Men only wanted sex, and women were
all resentful or jealous. Her parents seem to be professional
people living apart. She had no one to turn to.'

'Oh, come on, you'll be shedding tears next. This is a young
woman who milks men's vulnerability and flaunts it in front
of other women. Her promiscuous tendencies drove one
admirer to attack her, and she had no compunction in laying
the blame on another, knowing it would have serious consequences for him.'

'Mmm, the hardheaded policeman,' murmured Nora with a
hint of sadness. 'There's always a reason why people behave
as they do.'

'Yes, and the reason she behaved as she did is because she
gets her kicks from dangling men on a string until she lets
them drop with a painful thump. She's like Lorelei – sings
men towards their destruction.'

At that point, the brown puppy who had been sleeping
peacefully against Nora's soft slippers suddenly got to her
paws and ran to the front door.

'That'll be the girls.'

Tom wagged his head in wonderment. 'How does she always
know they're coming, even before they turn the corner?'

Nora grinned. 'She's the offspring of army dogs. What d'you
expect?'

Three minutes later there was the sound of lively voices
and excited yapping from Strudel. Considering it 'a bloody
stupid name for a dog' Tom invariably addressed the puppy
as 'tyke', which earned him protests and admonishing assaults
on his person from his daughters, which he secretly loved.
The house came alive as girls and small dog competed to be
heard, and Nora went to the kitchen to serve supper.

Holding back for a moment or two, Tom indulged once
more the prospect of Christopher Black joining their ranks.
A son, at last! What need had he of being stunned by a

fictional temptress when he had all he could want right
here?

In ten days it would be Easter. The March evening was balmy
enough to open the windows in the large room which separated
the two one-bedroom apartments, and was available for use
by both residents. Max and Clare both had the facility to lock
the door leading to their own premises, but tonight they were
eating supper at the extensive table designed for use when
they had guests.

Max had been keen to dine at Herr Blomfeld's inn to
compensate for the deferred reunion last night, but Clare said
she was tired after dealing with the casualties from the road
accident until the early hours, and would prefer to eat at home
where she could wear something loose and comfortable. While
he had been in Spain she had discovered a wonderful caterer
which would deliver hot meals to order, and she had regularly
taken advantage of the service.

'It's gourmet meals on wheels,' she told him as they had
parted after a light lunch in the Officers' Mess. 'Trust me.
You'll find these people a godsend. Forget frozen meals for
one. Their choice is astonishing. I'll place the order when I
get back to my office, and set a reasonable time for delivery.
We'll eat in the main lounge, and you can relax afterwards
while I play Grannie's piano. How does that sound?'

'As if you're determined I'll continue to convalesce.'

She had just laughed and said nothing more until he delivered
her to the Medical Centre. Climbing from his car, she pointed.

'That's the way to the main gate and the road leading home.
Get going!'

He had got going but, as Clare revealed as she served pork
cutlets with roasted vegetables and apple rings, then opened
the insulated container filled with thick savoury sauce, it had
not been in the direction of the main gate.

'You don't deserve pampering because you defied my orders
this afternoon. Duncan saw you leaving your headquarters half
an hour after I told you to go home.'

His niggling jealousy over the Scottish doctor made him demand whether she employed him as a spy. She silently held his gaze until he explained. 'My first visit the inquisitive major informed you of was due to the discovery that one of the casualties of the RTA you and he were involved with carried evidence of a warm relationship with Maria Norton. I was on my way home when I called in to pick up some notes from my office.

'Apparently, the missing girl is one of Signals' staff who deal with classified material. They are now worried about who she might have gone to on leaving the base, having been privy to something they consider to be highly sensitive. This puts a new slant on the case. The assault could have nothing to do with her pregnancy. She could have run from someone demanding that knowledge and trying to beat it out of her, which gives the case deeper significance. It also puts greater pressure on us to find her.'

Setting down her knife and fork, she said, 'Max, I know where this is leading. Tom and the team would have to deal with it if you were still in Spain.'

'But I'm *not*,' he replied emphatically. 'The situation is this. The team has on its hands the tasks of finding the perpetrator of a vicious attack on a female soldier, discovering who's waging a vengeful campaign against Phil Piercey, tracing the whereabouts of the victim who is battered, bruised and pregnant, and now they have to add the fact that she's a security risk. They need all the help they can get, and I intend to offer it.'

'What about the uniformed lads?'

'They have to make security arrangements for a group of senior officers arriving for talks with the West Wilts, who are coming in from Afghanistan tomorrow, and prepare plans for the Open Day on Easter Saturday when the base is open to the public. All that in addition to their normal patrols.'

Clare resumed eating. 'You mount a strong defence.'

Max decided to drop the subject, saying, 'You're right about the food. This is delicious. Is there a pudding?'

'Of course. Knowing men don't consider they've had a meal unless they've finished with something sweet and probably so solid it'll lay on their chest for most of the night, I ordered a fruity concoction light enough for me, but which comes with chocolate-covered ginger shortbreads. I'll generously bestow my share of them on you.'

'Bet it's because you don't like ginger shortbread.'

She sipped her wine. There was laughter in her blue eyes highlighted by the glow from candles in a branched holder that she had placed on the table. Studying her slender figure in a soft green plush kaftan, Max knew she lived up to the expectations he had had on deciding to leave her villa and attempt to clarify their relationship.

With Susan and Livya it had been instant and overwhelming attraction, which had not lasted for either of the women, but this love for Clare had come after they had been colleagues, neighbours and friends for nine months; had shared professional problems as well as pleasant, uncomplicated leisure times. In Spain his slow recovery had hampered the possibility of advancing their new closeness, but they had been at ease with each other because each knew the other in their every mood. For him, fondness had deepened slowly to make him aware that this time it was different. Lasting. He was fairly certain she felt that, too.

The meal finished, they poured the last of the wine and relaxed. Max settled in one of the deep armchairs by the window to listen while Clare played her grandmother's piano rescued from the wartime blitz. The wine, the music, the certainty of finally finding the future he had twice sought and lost induced in Max such desire for her he wondered how he would be able to deny it when the evening ended.

It happened sooner than he expected. After playing a lovely cascading impromptu which was a favourite of his, Clare closed the piano lid and stood.

'That's it! I'm too tired to continue, Max.'

He got to his feet, deeply disappointed. 'It's been a wonderful evening, like we used to have when you came over to Spain for a long weekend. This was even better because I'd waited so long to see you again.' He walked across to her. 'That's why I came back early. I'm sure you know that.'

She smiled up at him. 'I thought it was to escape Mollie Hubbard.'

It was not the response he had hoped for.

'Or to get back into harness with your detectives.'

While he feverishly struggled to think up the right words, she took his hand. 'If you want my approval for that you have to prove to me that you're now fully fit, and I know the perfect way for you to do that.' And she led him towards the door leading to her own apartment.

As so often happens, morning brought problems, created by the passion of the night before. Max had foreseen these weeks ago. He was unsure whether Clare had. Consequently, when he awoke at the usual time of six a.m. to find she was still sleeping he fought his instinct to wake her in the most satisfying way, slid from the bed, gathered his clothes and went to his own apartment, crossing the room where they had eaten last night. The dishes were still on the table; the candles had burned themselves out.

After an invigorating shower he dressed in a track suit, made tea and carried it back across the large room. Reaching her door he hesitated, then knocked quite firmly before entering the square hall off which her sizeable bed-sitting room lay, then on to the kitchen exactly like his own but in reverse. There was no sound from the main room, so he peered in. Clare was still asleep, but her alarm suddenly buzzed bringing her awake and aware of his figure at the doorway.

'I've made some tea,' he said from where he stood.

She smiled dreamily. 'And toast?'

'Can do.' Busy with the toaster, Max heard her shower running and was grateful that she had not stayed in bed. It would make what had to be said easier if they were well away from it. As he set out their breakfast he heard the hum of a hair drier and recalled that she had washed her hair in the shower every other morning during her brief visits to the Spanish villa. Feeling that the tea would be stewed by now, he made some fresh by which time she was standing beside him in her bathrobe, hair smelling of apples.

'You've used that shampoo that always reminds me of scrumping in a neighbouring orchard as a boy.'

She made a face. 'And you a future policeman!' Putting her arms around his neck she went on tiptoe to kiss him, quite thoroughly. 'Good morning, my fully fit and active friend. Pity we're not at the villa with a long, lazy day ahead.'

She sat on one of the tall stools and began buttering toast, the bathrobe parting enough to reveal her crossed legs. Max sat on the other stool, but ignored the food.

'Thank you for last night, Clare. You were very generous.'

She grew still, her knife deep inside the marmalade jar, and frowned. 'You make it sound as if I gave a performance for charity.'

Oh, God! He was making a dog's dinner of this; then he made it worse next minute. 'No, it's just that I need to get clear why. I mean, you said . . . well, I know that was . . . that you were joking . . .'

'You're asking if well and truly shagging a patient is one of my range of medical treatments? *No*, Max.'

'I'm asking if it was just a spur of the moment decision to end a wonderful evening.' Her subdued anger rid his mind of jumbled thoughts so he could tackle the issue clearly and concisely.

'I don't want to embark on a casual affair, tumbling into bed together now and again if we both feel in the mood. I've loved two other women. Neither of them were as fully committed as I was. I don't want a repetition with you.'

She put her hand over his which rested on the worktop, but he pressed on. 'I realized the depth of my feelings for you on the evening your ex tried to rape you, but next day I was blown up in a garden shed. Since then I've been in no condition to take things any further. Last night strengthened my belief that it could be possible.'

As she made to speak he hurried on. 'I wanted marriage, a real home and children with Livya Cordwell. She wanted those things with my father, not me. With Susan I almost had all three, and I choose to believe the child she was carrying was mine, not her lover's. I lost everything in a matter of minutes when she died beside him.

'I don't want sympathy, Clare,' he added sharply as she abandoned the toast and marmalade to put her other hand also on his. 'And I don't want to continue living here if your interest in me is transitory. I've always been a one-woman man. I don't do one night stands.'

Clare leaned forward to gaze steadfastly into his eyes. 'I fell in love with you on the night you jumped in the river to rescue a student.'

He could hardly believe what he was hearing. That incident had happened so early in their acquaintance.

'You were then beneath the spell of a woman who rated her career higher than she rated you, and I hid my jealousy better than you've hidden yours of Duncan MacPherson.' She squeezed his hand. 'If you're trying to say you want marriage, a real home and children with *me*, nothing would make me happier because it's what I want, too, darling.'

Wednesday brought the buzz of activity that always arose when troops were arriving back from Afghanistan. Those men and women who had spent six months in action in a warzone were returning to wives, husbands, lovers, children, houses or rooms in accommodation blocks which they regarded as home, and a normal routine which would seem almost unreal until the urgency, the sense of danger, the adrenalin-charged courage slowly drained away. It was not easy to adjust. Those who were single and uncommitted overcompensated for half a year without alcohol and sexual adventures, which kept the uniformed squad very busy.

However, a strict procedure had first to be carried out. All clothing, kit and weapons supplied for a Middle East sojourn had to be handed in and checked. The personal possessions of soldiers living in the accommodation blocks had to be collected from stores where they had been held securely during their absence, and regulation debriefing sessions were a priority before leave was granted.

The Drumdorran Fusiliers had moved into the base while the personnel of the West Wiltshire Regiment had been away, and the Bandmaster saw an opportunity to parade his beloved pipers for a musical welcome to the tanned, weary, stressed-out, saddened troops returning without eight of their number, two having been flown home in coffins a month earlier.

Tom, who hated the sound of bagpipes, declared it was more likely to cause the West Wilts to climb back in the coaches and return to face the Taliban, but he was in a minority of one and the familiar six-monthly turnaround became almost a party occasion, a huge crowd turning out on a beautiful sunny day to make merry. The stirring tunes played by the massed pipes, the musicians' kilts swinging, their plaids over their shoulders fluttering in the breeze, had spectators clapping to the drum-beat, and drove small boys and girls to march alongside them in delight.

The members of 26 Section continued their work of inter-viewing and eliminating every person who had even the frailest links with Maria Norton and the opera performances she had excelled in. They encountered much frustration. The musicians were parading around the base, and many people who had attended classes at the Recreation Centre on the same nights as rehearsals for *Carmen* were watching the band or embracing a loved one returning safely to them.

Connie Bush had better luck. Having been advised by a nurse at the private clinic that Staff Sergeant Andrews would not be brought from heavy sedation for another twelve hours, she had gone home for the night and revisited the patients after breakfast this morning. Andrews had still not emerged from sedation, so she talked to Sergeant Ted Griffiths about his two friends.

A lean, freckle-faced man with thinning light brown hair, the least injured of the three, he had a multitude of bruises which ranged from black through purple to blue and yellow, a broken toe and a four-inch laceration on his left leg.

'Talk about bloody luck,' he said to Connie, pointing to the other bed in the side room. 'My mates are well and truly mucked up. Only consolation is they won't remember anything about how it happened. I was out for a few minutes but, apart from that I saw and heard the whole appalling business.' He frowned. 'Wish I hadn't. It'll give me nightmares forever.' Responding to Connie's gift of encouraging confidences, he added, 'I mean, warfare's one thing. It's what we're trained for. But there were women and kids screaming out for help. And all that fire! Christ, it was like dying and arriving in hell.'

She nodded with understanding. 'I remember seeing as a child one of the thatched cottages in our village burning. It was the *sound* of flames roaring in the cold night air, the crackle and popping, like gunfire, that terrified me more than the fire itself. Fortunately there were a number of vehicles between yours and the centre of the pile-up on the autobahn. Have the *Polizei* visited to get a statement from you?'

He shook his head against the pillow. 'Once they realized who we were they were happy to get shot of us.'

Connie gave a faint smile. 'Sounds about right. Once all of you are fit to give an account we'll take notes and send a report to them. How's Sergeant Hibbert in Intensive Care? Have they told you the latest?'

'Yes, they're very good about that, even though they treat us like aliens from another planet most of the time. Hibby's doing OK. P'raps two more days, then he can join us. Trouble is, I'll be discharged by then and won't see him.'

'Surely they'll let you visit him before you leave.'

'No, Sarge, the only person allowed in there is his missus. They gave her a lounge chair with a pillow and blanket for the night.' He grimaced. 'She speaks good German. Probably gets better service.'

Thinking that the hospital visitor chatting had gone on long enough, Connie embarked on what she had really come for.

'Staff Andrews' wife and children in Ireland, have they been told about his condition?'

'Doubt it. When she upped and left, he saw the company commander and told him she was only to be notified if he was killed. Otherwise not. She really did the dirty on him. He hates her. I mean, really sodding *hates* her. But he misses the kids. Always sending money and presents. Never gets any replies, and they're all old enough to do that.' He gave a heavy shuddering sigh which was probably due to remnants of shock. 'On a hiding to nowhere, if you ask me. He's got no visiting rights, and she's a spiteful bitch who's likely poisoned their minds against their dad.'

'That's a shame,' murmured Connie, and meant it. Her own father and grandfather were killed in the light aircraft they had bought together and rejoiced in flying. She would give anything to have her dad back. 'Vince is fond of children, is he?'

'And some! He lived for his four.'

A fairly common story, thought Connie, although more often the other way round. 'So his wife tired of being ignored and looked elsewhere?'

Pale amber eyes studied her thoughtfully. 'You're a real surprise, know that?'

'In what way?' she asked, certain of his reply.

'Redcaps! Well, they're hard and mean. All brawn and not much else. But you. You're like a normal woman.'

She laughed softly. 'Oh, I can be hard and mean, Ted. Come up against me in a back alley on a dark night and you'd be sorry.'

It brought a return grin. 'I'd gladly meet you in a back alley on a dark night, if it wasn't for my girlfriend back home.'

'So Mrs Andrews had an affair while Vince spent all his time and energy on his kids?'

'No! She turned into a bloody saint; always in the church dusting and polishing and lighting candles. But for the kids she'd've taken vows and become a nun. No, it was Vince who had an affair. That didn't bother her for herself, but he'd sinned against the church which was more than she'd accept. So when Father Shannon suggested a short healing separation, she upped and decamped to Ireland and her devout family with every intention of staying there for good.'

Knowing she was getting the information she wanted, Connie was happy enough to be interrupted by a nurse who came to check on the condition of the man they were discussing, then to ask if they would like coffee.

'Soon he will be wakeful,' she told Connie as she left to fetch the drinks. 'But you must not make tired.'

Sipping her coffee gratefully, Connie asked, 'This affair of Vince's, is it still ongoing?'

'Ended very abruptly coupla months ago. Girl in Signals. Likes singing, so she gets the main part in some show and tells him she'll be too busy to be with him.'

'Was he upset?'

'*Upset*? Went ape when she told him that. I mean, it had been really hot. Vince was the happiest he'd been since Moira took the kids back to Ireland.'

'And now?'

Ted sighed. 'See, we three had long weekend passes, plans for a mini R and R but Vince, stupid bastard, was set on watching this girl strut her stuff on Saturday night. Couldn't budge him, so Hibbie and me said we'd have our usual pub crawl in town and stay overnight in a *Gasthof* that's not too fussy about the state you're in. We arranged to meet Vince at the Whirligig, but we bloody didn't track him down until three ack emma at Scarz. The bugger said he thought that was the agreed RV, but he was pretty much legless and we guessed he'd been drowning his sorrows after seeing her again. Mind you, we were also well pissed by then.'

He gave a grin cheeky enough to suggest it was normally like that. 'We got him to the digs. Hibs and me took the beds and made Vince a bivvy on the floor in case he threw up. Next day we walked the track from here to Kitzdorf, right along the crest of the range, bedding down in the log cabin on Sunday night before taking the valley walk back to where we'd left the car.'

'How did Vince seem at that stage?' Connie asked.

'Quiet, depressed, anti-women, which Hibbs and me thought a good thing.' His vitality suddenly drained away, the amber eyes glassed over. 'We were bringing him home when that tanker skidded into the gas bottles and . . .' He could not continue, and tears began sliding down his cheeks. 'Those women and kids screaming for help. I'll never forget that.'

There was silence between them for a moment or two, until a mutter from the other bed told Connie Vince Andrews had re-entered the conscious world.

The late afternoon briefing added very little to progress the case. Only half the Drumdorran musicians had been successfully pinned down long enough to question their actions following the final curtain last Saturday. All of them had solid alibis. A few of the backstage crew had also been interviewed and cleared of suspicion.

Private Jimmy James had told Heather he was *almost* sure the car outside the gymnasium had been the same shape as Norton's Clio, but he could be mistaken. Piercey's computerized list of red vehicles registered to owners living on the base showed no Clio or any other car that was a similar shape. On being approached again, Jimmy James had said he was *almost* sure the car had been red, but he could be mistaken.

Piercey was disgusted. 'I told you he could identify down to the last stitch a three-piece suit. At a stretch he might know the size of a man's sock, but he sees everything else through closed lids. His claim to have watched my car being driven away ten minutes after I arrived at the Mess has to be totally discounted.'

'He's not dozy enough to imagine it,' Simpson pointed out. 'We either have to chase up another witness or find out who might have left the Mess in the early hours, because somebody drove off ten minutes after you arrived there.'

Piercey found this theory attractive. 'That opens up a new avenue, because he could have been the bloke Maria was calling in the dressing room, then called again while Bill

Jensen was agitating about locking up. He could have gone to meet her and consequently beat her up.'

Heather nodded. 'And the vehicle outside the gymnasium that Jimmy James saw on his lonely walk could be just a red herring.'

'Or he could be mistaken,' added Beeny dryly. 'I think we need to eliminate some of these vague leads. What Phil says makes a deal of sense. The timing would be right. Chummy's waiting in his room in the Mess for her call, but it's interrupted by Phil who believes she's going with him to the Black Bear. Norton calls again after everyone leaves and Bill's rattling his keys impatiently. The rendezvous's fixed during that second call. Norton drives there from the Recreation Centre and Chummy goes to meet her ten, fifteen minutes after Phil arrives in such a temper he leaves his Audi unlocked, giving Chummy the perfect opportunity to dump Norton's mobile in there after he's attacked her.'

'Sounds feasible,' said Tom thoughtfully. 'Staff Andrews has been living in the Mess since his wife took the family back to Ireland.' He turned to Connie. 'Does that theory fit with what you learned at the clinic?'

'It could. Andrews himself was still very muzzy. I couldn't get much out of him, and the nurse more or less ordered me to leave. I'd been there almost two hours before he regained consciousness, so she wanted me out of the way. However, Ted Griffiths was so glad to have someone to talk to I merely had to steer him in the right direction to get the info I wanted.

'According to him, Norton had a hot affair with Staff Andrews but broke it off two months ago when she took on the role of Carmen; told him she had to concentrate on her singing.' Her eyebrows rose. 'Ted said his mate "went ape" at first, then appeared to come to terms with it until he stupidly went to see the opera on Saturday night. This messed up the three-day walking break Ted, Sarn't Hibbert and Andrews had forward planned, but the other two were generous enough to agree to have their usual Saturday booze-up, then begin the hiking on Sunday morning after overnighting in town. Staff

Andrews was deeply depressed and uncommunicative during the walk in the hills, Ted told me. They were returning on Monday night when they were smashed up in the RTA.

'I was unable to get confirmation of any of this from Staff. In fact, he seemed so disorientated I wondered if he had suffered slight brain damage. The nurse said no, but he might have no memory of the accident and what happened shortly beforehand. I'll go back in the morning when he's had time to get his thoughts together.

'I've been mulling over what Ted told me and come up with a theory of my own.' Tom's nod encouraged her to continue. 'Norton ended the affair two months ago when rehearsals for *Carmen* began. The timing ties in with the discovery that she's pregnant, and so she arranged a meeting with the father to give him the news. Unless she was having sex with others, Staff Andrews must surely be responsible for her condition.'

Piercey could not help butting in. 'She certainly wasn't having it off with anyone during those two months. I can vouch for that, along with half a dozen others,' he added sourly.

'The fact that his pals had to RV with him in town when they usually all set out together casts doubt on his movements at the end of Saturday's performance. He might well have been legless when they caught up with him, but he could have been tanking up in his room in the Mess while waiting for Norton's call. If he had been it would account for the viciousness of the attack on her, and also explain why he took a taxi into town. The car that was smashed up belonged to Hibbert. There was no mention of them leaving one to be picked up once Andrews sobered up.'

Tom smiled at her. 'Good work, sharp thinking. I suggest we call it a day and develop that scenario tomorrow. Another check with taxi firms will give us the time Andrews was picked up, unless he hailed one outside the base.' He ended by giving them the results of his enquiries. 'The trail on Norton has gone cold. I contacted both parents, but they had not spoken to their daughter for several weeks and couldn't suggest any friend or relative she might have gone to in trouble.

'My only reservation on this new line is that nobody we

questioned mentioned a hot affair between the two. Or of Norton with anyone else, come to that. Hot it might have been, but they must have used excessive discretion to keep it so utterly secret.'

'She works in that mode,' mused Simpson. 'Maybe she applies it to every aspect of her life.'

'Huh! She made no secret of how she operates to every male in that opera,' Piercey said bitterly. 'I see now it was to hide what she was really up to with Staff Andrews.'

Glaring at Piercey, Tom said, 'Norton's mobile phone provider is being obstructive about giving us info on the phone number of the last people she called. They're saying the contract was cancelled on Monday so all records concerning it had probably been wiped. Chummy appears to have thought of everything, unless Norton herself took steps to prevent us from tracing whoever she's protecting with her false accusation.'

SEVEN

Max's non-appearance on Wednesday led Tom to believe Clare Goodey's strictures had persuaded him to stick to the rules until passed fit by the Medical Board. Paradoxically, he missed the input of a man who often saw a different interpretation of plain facts which sometimes furthered a case. On the other hand, it often clouded the issue. He went home to Nora and his family believing he must do without Max's help in getting to grips with the ever growing complications surrounding Corporal Maria Norton.

Tom was wrong. After the momentous discovery that the future he so much wanted was there to grasp, Max sat for an hour or so after Clare left to take the morning sick parade and allowed his imagination full rein. A home. A *real* home. A property with enough rooms for children to occupy and grow up in; one which he and Clare owned, not rented. A house that would reflect both their personalities. They would also have the villa in Spain. Everything was possible now.

By mid-morning he was sitting at the desk in his own apartment, making notes on the Norton case from copies of the team's reports he had collected before leaving the base yesterday afternoon. There were by now so many facets he decided to concentrate on the one which concerned him the most, and he spent several hours catagorizing paragraphs from statements in order to get a clear assessment of known facts.

In the afternoon he undertook another task which he intended to reveal to Clare at the end of the day. Before that they were to have the meal at the riverside inn they liked so much which they should have had on Monday. They had no sooner been shown to the table he had reserved than Herr Blomfeld arrived with a bottle of champagne.

'Please to accept with my goodest wishes for both,' he said, popping the cork and pouring the sparkling wine in two glasses he had brought with him. 'I have never forget the pulling from the river the young woman who could die. You are special from then. Now even more special to have the bombing and again come to this place,' he added looking at Max. 'I am most thankful.'

Max was embarrassed. The words were clearly heartfelt, so he responded appropriately, but he was glad when Blomfeld walked away wreathed in smiles.

'What a sweetie,' said Clare.

'Doubtless he had planned that for Monday, but you called my mobile and put an end to it. I was so upset I drove off without giving him an explanation. Just left.'

'That won't happen tonight now we've left our mobiles at home.' She smiled at him as she raised her glass. '*Prost!*'

On sudden impulse Max put out his hand and gently eased hers back to the table. 'I planned this for when we got home but you look so lovely, we're at the place where you claim to have realized your true feelings for me, and we have a bottle of celebration champagne, so this seems the right moment.'

Taking from his pocket the box containing a sapphire and diamond ring he had bought four hours ago, he pushed it across the table. 'I'd really like to drive around shouting the news through a loud hailer, but you'd probably prefer this method of announcing that you've agreed to become my wife.'

Flushed and obviously taken by surprise, Clare opened the velvet box, then looked up. 'Max, it's beautiful. *Beautiful!*'

'I'm afraid I invaded your apartment to borrow one of your rings to get the size right.'

As she slid the ring on the third finger of her left hand, Max noticed that it was bare. 'You've taken off Goodey's wedding band!'

Her eyes grew bright with affection. 'I can be a fast worker too. I ditched it before I left for work this morning: no longer need the phoney protection it provided.'

He gripped her hand. 'How soon can I replace it?'

'Tomorrow seems a bit quick. How about the day after?'

she teased. Picking up her glass again she said softly, 'Here's to us, darling, and our golden future.'

When Max walked in the next morning Tom could not hide his surprise. 'I thought the Doc read you the riot act on Tuesday.'

'I persuaded her my contribution to the case wouldn't be strenuous enough to cause a medical relapse,' he replied with a grin. 'I'm concentrating on the mental detective work, as our revered Regional Commander suggested, and I've come up with an interesting theory.' He laughed. 'No, Tom, there's not a wild goose flapping its wings, I promise. Let's discuss it over coffee and a bun.'

Standing by the whiteboard with their favourite sustenance, Max began on his theory based on the work he had done yesterday morning. 'Piercey left the theatre at oh one ten and reached the Mess at oh one thirty. Private Jimmy James witnessed his arrival then saw the Audi depart again at oh one forty.' He wrote all this on the board as he spoke. 'Norton made a call on her mobile in her dressing room at oh one five which Piercey interrupted. She made another, presumably to the same person, prior to leaving at oh one fifteen. She staggered into the RMP Post at oh two hundred. Allowing for a reasonable time to elapse between the assault and her arrival at the Post, it means around thirty minutes are unaccounted for.

'Now, if Phil is innocent we're presented with some interesting possibles. The idea of someone borrowing the Audi for some nefarious business we know nothing about is surely negated by the discovery of Norton's mobile having been planted in it with all but Phil's texts deleted. So, the events of that night were almost certainly conceived to damage him quite seriously, and that only works if the plan included a crime for which he could be blamed.'

He raised his eyebrows at Tom. 'With me so far? Right. Chummy could only know Phil's movements after the opera party if Norton told him. Which means she must have been in on the plan, which includes making a fuss in the theatre to drive Phil to leave in a hurry. She then phones Chummy so that he can watch for his arrival at the Mess. Phil carelessly leaves the keys in the ignition, but Chummy would have provided himself in advance with the means of breaking into it. Easy when you know how.

'Here's my theory. Norton is told the plan is to tell the Redcaps Phil laid in wait for her to arrive at her accommodation block, forced her into his car, drove away from the built up area, then tried to rape her in the vehicle.'

'But Chummy had other plans,' said Tom, catching the drift. 'She did all they'd agreed to, but he knocked her about instead of simply tearing her dress and mussing her hair.'

'Exactly! Norton was in shock when Babs Turvey asked what had happened, so she named Phil, as arranged.'

'And she was still so shocked when I interviewed her on Sunday she couldn't remember the rehearsed script and made up a wild story to support her allegation.'

Max nodded. 'By the following day she realized the enormity of what was happening and ran.' He drank some coffee, then pulled a face. 'Should have drunk this before I began, when it was hot.'

Tom was still looking thoughtful. 'I agree the theory fits the timing and the facts we have, but it leaves loose ends. The main one is why?'

'I've no idea,' Max confessed. 'I suggest we put it to Piercey and the rest of the team. It might connect with something way back when Phil tangled with Chummy.'

'Why wait so long for revenge?'

'Oh, you know how it happens. Resentment builds and grows out of proportion as it festers. Then a perfect opportunity comes along. Phil makes a public idiot of himself over Norton, and bingo! A charge of attempted rape is a serious enough crime to ruin a career and earn a prison sentence.'

'Mmm, Norton's reputed power over men would have been reversed if we believe that scenario.'

Max smiled. 'Even our womanizer Piercey succumbed eventually, became putty in a woman's hands. Norton must have fallen really hard for someone who could persuade her to do whatever he asked.'

'The father of her baby?'

'Who knows, but she's frightened enough of him now to run away.'

'Or she's frightened of what he's led her into. Connie mentioned Sharmayne Parker who still defended her abusive lover when we arrested him. Women do that quite frequently. Norton could well have been trying to contact her lover from that eaterie. Bugger, *I'm* calling it that now,' Tom said tetchily.

'If only we could get Deutsche Telecom to give us the number she contacted three times. Presumably she was trying to speak to whoever should have been waiting for her in the Imperial Hotel.'

At that point they realized the team had assembled and coffee was being made. Armed with refills Max let Tom outline what they had been discussing, and ask for input firstly from Piercey.

True to character the Cornish sergeant asked, 'So I'm no longer regarded as guilty?'

Tom said coldly, 'I haven't heard anyone say that, have you?'

Piercey never knew when to stop. 'But you're saying I was deliberately set up by Norton and her lover?'

Max intervened hastily. 'It's one possible theory, that's all. You've been accused of assault. It's been officially recorded and will stand until we have indisputable proof of your innocence. We don't yet have that. Now answer Mr Black's question. Can you offer any insight on possible encounters past or present which could cause someone to plan this kind of revenge?'

'Christ, I don't know how squaddies' mind's work,' he said explosively. 'They all hate our guts. It'd only take a few beers and several brainless mates to set one of them up for something like that.'

'We're not talking about squaddies,' snapped Tom. 'They'd corner you in a dark alley and beat you senseless. What we're

considering here is a clever plan with careful timing designed
to get you a serious police record. Chummy wanted more than
a punch-up, he wanted to damage your entire future.'

Reminded of this threat, Piercey dropped his aggressive
stance. 'I can't think of any incident that would account for
that depth of revenge, sir. For four days and nights I've racked
my brains for a reason why that woman has done this to me,
and I still can't understand it.'

'But if this new theory is near enough right it's Chummy
who's punishing you, isn't it?' reasoned Beeny. 'Norton was
just a pawn in his game.'

Heather Johnson said somewhat tartly, 'What about the
women you've been around with, if you can possibly remember
them all? One of them may well now know Chummy as well
as she once knew you and saw a means of getting even with
you.'

'For *what*?' cried Piercey. 'I'm sick and tired of your snide
comments on my private life. Every relationship I've had has
been fully consensual. There's nothing for any woman to *get
even* for.'

Tom was furious. 'You're supposed to be detectives
reviewing a serious and complicated case, not cats fighting on
a rooftop. If that's the best you can come up with, Sergeant
Johnson, you'd better keep quiet.'

Not to be outdone, she said, 'The case concerns someone
conspiring against Phil. We've been acting on the belief that
Norton was the prime mover, so why couldn't it have been
another woman who instigated it? If we're now considering
Chummy to have some need to discredit Phil, surely it's
feasible that an ex-girlfriend presently deeply involved with
him could be using him as *her* pawn.'

Max intervened again, relieving Tom of the obligation of
following up on that. 'It's an outside possibility, but it would
cloud the issue further if, at this stage, we seriously investigated
it. The case is complicated enough. Let's stick with the original
scenario for now.'

Into the silence caused by no further input being offered,

Olly Simpson said in his unflappable manner, 'There's another way of looking at this. It seems pretty certain the theory of conspiracy between Norton and a male friend is correct. She's besotted enough to do anything he asks and possibly sees this campaign against Phil as an expression of her lover's jealousy, which she finds exciting. Norton does exactly as directed, phones to say Phil has left the theatre, then goes to meet Chummy at the agreed rendezvous where he attacks her as brutally as he has planned to do.'

He leaned back and folded his arms behind his head. 'His revenge was against Norton. *Phil* was the pawn.'

They all looked at Simpson, struck by this twist to the concept. Then Piercey said eagerly, 'She could have been told to play that game with any one of us she'd been coming-on to over those two months of rehearsals.'

Simpson nodded. 'Unfortunately, you drew the short straw. Maybe she mentioned your name more than the others.'

'Or because of who you are,' put in Beeny. 'An opportunity to get one in against the law and order lads. Just for fun!'

Tom glanced at Max, then said, 'That's a working possibility which leaves us with two options. Chummy is the father of Norton's baby and stages this whole thing to cover the hiding he means to give her for refusing the abortion. *Or* she's told him she's pregnant by another man and he gives her a violent farewell knowing she's not likely to shop him because she'd have to confess to conspiring to set up an innocent man as a rapist. That's why she ran. However, none of these theories gives us a clue to Chummy's identity.'

'How about Staff Andrews?' suggested Connie, who had been quietly assessing all this speculation. 'His hot affair, which nobody seems to have been aware of, was terminated by Norton when she began rehearsing for *Carmen* two months ago. She's two months pregnant. He arranges to be at the Recreation Centre on rehearsal nights, maybe sees Phil hanging around her too much and starts to smoulder.'

Beeny challenged that. 'Why would Norton conspire with a man she'd discarded?'

'If the affair had been hot enough he could have reignited it when she revealed she was carrying his baby. Andrews is known to adore his four children who're now in Ireland with his wife's family who've all poisoned their minds against him, he reckons. The thought of another child of his own would drive him to ensure they got back together. Norton is known to relish men's adoration. He could play on that to the hilt, and she'd most probably fall for it.

'He attended the opera performance on Saturday. He lives in the Sergeants' Mess and returns there to wait for Norton's call saying Phil is on his way. He watches his quarry enter in a foul mood, waits ten minutes, then drives the Audi to Norton's accommodation block to pick her up.' She frowned in concentration. 'Why would he assault her, though?'

'She has last minute reservations. Doesn't want to go through with it; retracts all she's told him about Phil's frequent attempts to get her into bed, which she has exaggerated to make Andrews jealous,' said Heather. 'He loses it. Gives her a going over and dumps her near the RMP Post.'

Connie nodded. 'Then he returns Phil's car, plants her mobile in it, and sets out for town where his mates finally track him down in the early hours, completely legless. They put up for the night, then follow their plan to walk the track to Kitzdorf and back along the valley. They're returning to base on Monday evening when they get caught in that pile-up on the autobahn. As of now he's unaware that Norton's gone into hiding.'

'And also unaware that she's accused Phil, as they had arranged. Once he regains full consciousness he'll start to worry,' mused Heather. 'Worry whether she's landed him in it after all.'

Tom regarded the grouped members of the team, asking, 'Any more variations on an original theme?' Silence. 'You're due to visit Staff Andrews again, Connie. Question him bearing in mind what you've just outlined. With one or two question marks I think it's quite sound.' He turned to Max. 'Anything to add, sir?'

Before Max could answer, his mobile rang showing the call

was from Clare. Connecting, he said quietly, 'I'll call you asap.'

'I think you'll want to hear this, Captain Rydal.'

So it was business, not pleasure. 'Go ahead.'

'We've just received a call from the hospital. Corporal Maria Norton has been admitted as an emergency. Haemorrhaging from an unprofessional abortion.'

Lieutenant Su Carfax was in her office when Max called in at 5 Signals Headquarters. She glanced up as he entered and Max was again struck by her arresting, exotic beauty. He could not help thinking she ought to be a couturier's model, an actress, a tycoon's PA rather than a soldier dressed in combats and heavy boots.

'You have news of Corporal Norton?' she asked swiftly.

He nodded. 'We're on our way to the hospital to question her.'

She got to her feet in alarm. 'How bad is it?'

'We won't know exactly until we speak to the doctors, but Captain Goodey didn't consider there'd be any risk to her life now she's receiving medical attention.'

The subaltern came around her desk, black eyes full of concern. 'Was she attacked again?'

'That's what we have to discover. The MO was told she was haemorrhaging from a bungled abortion when a local woman came across her in the toilets at Gunters, and informed the staff. They called an ambulance right away. I suppose you could say she had been attacked – by some kind of rusty, blunt instrument, I imagine.'

His companion shuddered with horror and looked very upset. 'Why didn't she come to me before it all went wrong? I've always made it clear I'm available to talk over any problems, help in any way open to me. Other girls have benefited that way.'

Preparing to rejoin Connie who was waiting in his car, Max said, 'Everyone we've questioned so far has said Maria Norton is very self-assured, has very definite ideas on how to run her life, which suggests that that changed on Saturday night when someone violently assaulted her. It's important to discover whether she tried to terminate her pregnancy under duress or of her own free will. It's *essential* that we learn the identity of the potential father. She refused to name him when Mr Black questioned her after the assault. We can move forward swiftly once we know his identity.'

They were now both walking along the corridor, the woman beside him still looking deeply disturbed, when Max said, 'If you can throw any light here you *must* tell us.'

She angled her face so that she looked away through the row of windows. 'I've already said she didn't take advantage of my offer of help.'

He stepped forward and turned to block her advance, obliging her to halt. 'You know very well what I mean, Miss Carfax. Norton was privy to a highly confidential and, I suspect, damaging transmission at noon on Saturday. Twelve hours later she was brutally beaten. It doesn't take abnormal intelligence to work out that someone might have been trying to make her reveal that info. Or ensure that she never passed it on.'

Carfax attempted to avoid the issue with a light laugh. 'You sound like a character in a cheap espionage thriller.'

'I'll sound even more like one by saying there's a chance that you could become the next victim of violence if that transmission *is* at the core of this case.'

He could not miss the significance of the obstinate pursing of that petal mouth, and the fire in her eyes which indicated her refusal to cooperate.

'You were worried enough to come to us yesterday and put probing questions about what we might have learned from Norton. If that transmission was sensitive enough to have you all running around like headless chickens because of what happened to the woman who authenticated it, we need to know.'

She shook her head vigorously. 'It doesn't work like that.'

'OK, after we've seen Norton, if I think it's relevant I'll

speak to your Squadron Commander, Major Evans.' At the head of the flight leading down to where his car stood, he added, 'Just watch your step and keep clear of dark, lonely places meanwhile.'

He had passed through the main gate, driven the length of the feeder road and was several miles along the autobahn before Connie attempted to break the silence.

'How likely d'you think some damning communication could be at the root of this curious affair, sir?'

Almost at the crossroads where he must turn right, Max sighed. 'I hope to God it isn't, because it would have to be evidence of villainy involving a group of disparate people, one of whom is Phil Piercey. An hour or so ago we worked out three possible scenarious woven around a small nucleus of evidence. I'd be happy to prove any one of them to be fact, but start dabbling in classified, need-to-know info and things become very sticky indeed.'

He indicated and turned on to the road leading to the hospital. 'The one thing I'm certain of is that it'll take a determined inquisition to break through the silence of the main players before we trace the spark that set this trail ablaze.'

Tom decided to call in for a mid-morning snack with Nora before heading for the private clinic where Staff Sergeant Andrews should have recovered his senses enough to be questioned in depth. Nora had been for a routine check on the position of the baby, certain that he would be arriving earlier than expected. Having had three, she claimed young Christopher Black was too robust to wait much longer to join them. Bearing in mind the worrying period they had had at the same late stage with Gina, Tom was anxious to hear what Clare Goodey had had to say on the subject.

Much as he longed to hear that first lusty cry, and hold his son in his arms, he had concerns about a premature birth. Nora seemed unfazed but, like many prospective fathers, Tom always felt isolated from the mysteries of pregnancy. He could never know what Nora felt, never know the pain of giving birth.

Only when the infant emerged, an amazing tiny human being, could he then fully share what they had created together.

He parked in the driveway and hurried to put his key in the lock of the front door. As it opened he heard a baby crying and his heart missed a beat. More than one, surely, so great was the shock. Why had they failed to call him? Why had it happened here? Why were there no other cars outside?

His wife was in the kitchen soothing an infant who sat on one of the stools while having a small cut on her finger dabbed free of a blister of blood with a tissue.

Nora glanced up with a smile of welcome. 'Hallo! Now, Lily, here's a handsome prince come unexpectedly to save you from the nasty dragon who bit your finger. Show him how brave you are. Not as brave as he is, of course, but a little girl who never makes a fuss even when it *really* hurts.'

Tom sighed with relief. How many times had they played that game with their three? 'Where is the dragon?' he demanded gruffly. 'Shall I need my sword?'

The child gazed at him wide-eyed and slowly shook her head. Nora spoke for her. 'Strudel chased it away. He wasn't a very good dragon, was he, to be afraid of a puppy?'

The fantasy was thankfully interrupted by the doorbell announcing the arrival of Mummy, and Tom was left to switch on the kettle then fill the cafetière, cursing himself for imagining the cries of an eighteen-month-old were like those of a newborn baby.

Nora returned having restored Lily to her mother. 'Met Glenda Pocock at the antenatal clinic. Duncan MacPherson sent her to the hospital for another scan; some problem with the baby's position. I offered to look after Lily. Hospital appointments are a misery with a toddler who insists on going walkabout. As it was, Lily pricked her finger on a rose bush and saw blood! Enough to set her screaming for Glenda.' She poured boiling water in the cafetière. 'What are you here for – apart from chasing dragons?'

Tom took her in his arms and kissed her with the verve of his concern and gratitude. She gazed questioningly at him when they drew apart.

'What was that all about?'

He touched her cheek with gentle fingers. 'It's about you being my wife, the mother of our children and the person who makes life so good for us all.' He settled her on a stool. 'Sit there while I pour coffee and listen to what the Doc said about your theory on Christopher's early arrival.'

'She's inclined to believe someone who's produced three to her none. Wants me back in a week rather than two. Tom, there's nothing to worry about, I promise.'

He pushed a mug of coffee towards her. 'OK, if you say so.'

'I wouldn't keep anything from you however bad, you know that.'

He helped himself to a slice of fruit cake. 'I'll just be glad when it's over and we can settle in the new routine.'

'Won't we both,' she agreed heartily. Biting into a biscuit, she asked, 'Have you seen Max today?'

He nodded. 'Can't keep him away.'

'Has he said anything to you?'

'About officially resuming command?'

'About his personal life.'

'His personal life?'

Nora grinned. 'Clare Goodey is wearing a very pretty diamond and sapphire ring on the third finger of her left hand. Unless she's been keeping a lover well out of sight, I'd say Max finally came to his senses and recognized they're made for each other.'

'She's been seen off base with that kilted doctor she works with, when Max was in Spain.'

'No, it's definitely Max,' she said firmly. 'If Livya Cordwell hadn't been on the scene when Clare arrived here this would have happened sooner.'

'Well, well! Wonder how long it'll be before he gives out the news. Everyone on the base will know by tomorrow evening.'

'Yes. She's clearly keen to show off her ring to all her patients and, presumably, to her fellow officers when she lunches in the Mess. June wedding?'

Tom gave a knowing smile. 'Providing there's not a juicy case to investigate. He'd hate to miss out on it.'

EIGHT

E ven in his bruised and lacerated state it was possible for Tom to see that Staff Sergeant Andrews would normally cut a dashing figure. His muscular build, dark curling hair and deep blue eyes would attract the girls, but a wife and four children in Ireland would surely put a damper on lasting passion. Small wonder Maria Norton chose her passion for singing as the better option.

Andrews was not happy to see Tom. Resting against piled pillows, he said, 'Where's that bonny girl who came yesterday?'

Tom ignored that and moved up to stand at the head of the bed, which gave him the advantage of rearing above Andrews. He had little doubt Connie had sat beside him for her distinctive persuasive questioning, but the patient was now conscious enough to face hard facts. Ted Griffiths was in the day room watching TV while waiting for his discharge documents. His bed in that double room had already been stripped ready for the next patient to book in.

'I want you to tell me in fullest detail your movements last Saturday, Staff. I've spoken to the doctor. He says full recollection of the time shortly before the accident could have returned.'

'It hasn't. He told *me* I might never remember those hours just before Hibbs' car hit the pile-up ahead of us. Ted told me he's off the critical list now. Is that right?' he asked urgently.

'Yes. I checked his condition with the doctor before I came in to you.'

Andrews looked genuinely relieved. 'Good! Me and Hibbs've been mates a long, long time.'

'It's not the hours just prior to the accident I'm interested in,' Tom said, sensing an attempt to avoid being interviewed. 'Tell me about Saturday, two days before the mental block.'

Andrews studied the facing wall. 'It's all a blur. *Everything's* a blur. I've been in a coma, you know.'

'Now you're out of it and making good progress. That's the medical prognosis as of fifteen minutes ago,' Tom said sharply. 'We can do this the easy or the hard way, the easy way being that you answer my questions fully and honestly.' He drew in his breath before adding, 'The hard way being that, in the face of your feigned amnesia, I go ahead and arrest you on suspicion of violent assault on Corporal Maria Norton and leaving her in an isolated area having deprived her of any means of summoning medical help.'

'*What?*' he cried. 'Are you on the up and up, or is this an SIB tactic to get a confession?' Seeing Tom's expression, he looked really distressed. 'You're saying someone beat her up? Oh God, how bad is she?' As Tom remained silent, he asked fearfully, 'Is she dying?'

It was clear to Tom's experienced eyes that this was the first Vince Andrews knew of what had befallen the young corporal over the past few days. If he was the father of the aborted foetus he had further bad news to face.

'She's presently in the hospital in town and should make a full recovery.' He now pulled up a chair and settled back to hear facts that would surely exonerate Andrews, but hopefully give a lead to the real perpetrator.

Not far off tears, Vince Andrews said, 'We had something going. Not your one-night stand. A real relationship. Met up at the Mess Christmas do. Sarn't Peake brought her, but I took her home. It was that quick. For us both. Weeks went by while I was thinking how to get around to the fact I was still married. Legal separation isn't divorce. Maria's Catholic, like my wife, so she understood and was happy to go on as we were.'

'Until when?' Tom asked, already knowing the answer.

Andrews pulled a tissue from a box on the bedside locker and blew his nose noisily. 'Out of the blue she tells me she's got the lead part in some show the Operatic Society was putting on, so she'll be spending all her free time on rehearsals, and lessons with a retired opera singer in town.' He frowned at

Tom. 'Just like that. Curtain down. Show over! I thought she was joking. Teasing.'

'But she wasn't?'

He slowly shook his head. 'It took a week for it to sink in. I mean, we were that close.'

'Did you attempt to restart the affair?'

'You know how it is. You keep hoping,' he said in man to man fashion. 'I went to the Recreation Centre a coupla nights when they were rehearsing. Stood at the back where no one would notice me. Shook me how good she was. Fantastic voice!' He paused, back to staring at the facing wall. 'After that second time I gave up hoping.' He looked back at Tom. 'What she was doing on stage to the bloke who was supposed to be guarding her was what she did with me. It was all an act. Switched on and off. She'd never meant any of it.'

'That made you angry?'

'With myself,' Andrews told the bedcover. 'Bloody fool she'd made me.'

Tom shifted position on the hard chair. 'Can we now get to your movements on Saturday night?'

Andrews seemed to suddenly recollect why he was being questioned by SIB, because he snapped out a denial that he had attacked Maria.

'So tell me what you were doing at the time of the attack, Staff,' Tom responded in similar crisp tones. 'Ted Griffiths has given evidence that he and Sarn't Hibbert agreed to delay the proposed hiking break until Sunday, and arranged to meet you in town for the usual pub crawl. Is that right?'

The brief aggression died. Andrews sighed heavily and blew his nose again. Tom saw the man was tiring, so he decided to let him tell it without interruption and in his own time. The first few minutes of his statement just confirmed what Ted had told Connie. Andrews had not been able to resist a last chance of seeing Norton perform. Twisting the knife?

'Dressed in that Spanish costume, with everyone else in full theatrical gear and with a full orchestra, she was *brilliant*. And that dying scene! I was . . . well, I was bowled over worse than before. I just had to see her again. I knew there was a party for cast and friends afterwards, so instead of going to town I went back to the Mess and tried to phone her. I'd almost given up when she finally answered, but I heard a man's voice in the background and she told me she'd ring back in ten.'

This all tied in with Piercey's evidence and Tom felt he was finally getting somewhere with the case.

'Well, she didn't,' Andrews said, 'but she had sounded so friendly before she was interrupted I decided to drive to her accommodation block and wait for her there. It must have been only five or so minutes before her Clio came round the corner and pulled up in her parking spot.

'I was on the point of getting out to cross to her when another vehicle careered round the corner, skidded to a halt, and she bloody ran and got in it! It shot off again like someone was chasing it, and I was so pissed off I decided to follow and see where they were heading.'

'And?' Tom asked sharply.

'He stopped on the road a few yards from the copse. I thought they were going in there for some shagging in the hut by the barbecue area, but they started at it in the bloody car. The way it was rocking they were so crazy they couldn't wait to get at it.' His mouth twisted in disgust. 'I left them to it and drove out to the repair shop where I'd arranged to leave my 4by4 on the forecourt. They're Jewish; work on Sundays. I'd planned to pick it up on Monday evening. I guess Isaac is wondering when I'm coming for it,' he ended heavily.

'Give me the details and I'll see to it,' Tom told him, deciding to keep to himself the probability that the rampant sex Andrews thought was making the vehicle rock was really caused by the vicious attack on the girl who had climbed so eagerly in beside her attacker.

Now came the vital question. 'Did you see who was driving the car?'

'Too dark. I memorized the reg number meaning to check it out.'

He recited the number of Piercey's Audi.

Max's first impression of Maria Norton was of a young woman with a mass of black hair surrounding a white face blotched with vivid brusing, whose dark eyes gazed blankly appearing to register nothing of her surroundings. He and Connie could have been invisible as they stood beside her bed around which a nurse had drawn blue floral curtains for privacy.

Max found all he had heard about the strong sexual allure of this army corporal difficult to imagine; she looked pathetically vulnerable and . . . yes, *scared*. Holding back, he motioned Connie to pull out the chair and adopt her usual persuasive techinque in the hope of breaking through the cocoon of misery.

'Maria, I'm Connie Bush and my companion is Captain Rydal. We're from SIB, and we've come to help you sort things out. Everything that's happened to you over the past few days. You're probably feeling very low. I can understand that. It's a woman's natural reaction to having an abortion, especially if she had to make the decision on her own. Is that what happened, Maria? Or did the father insist on it? Perhaps you wanted to have the baby.'

There was no response. Not even a flicker of reaction in those deep, dark eyes.

'Why didn't you talk to Lieutenant Carfax about it? She's always prepared to offer advice, or simply listen. We all need to talk things through with someone now and again.'

Still no response.

'Can you tell me where you went for the abortion? Who gave you the details? The father of the baby?'

Connie glanced up at Max, then turned back to embark on a new approach. 'Everyone on the base is still talking about your great performance in *Carmen*. I understand the Bandmaster is eager for you to sing at their concerts. I'm sure there'd be no official opposition to that. What an opportunity to use that lovely voice you have. Great success in the opera, the offer to sing in public with the Drumdorrans, and Su Carfax told me you're in line for promotion to sergeant. Everything going for you.' She allowed a short pause. 'So why did you turn your back on the Army, Maria?'

Max decided to follow up on that theme, saying quietly, 'You were on duty on Saturday when a highly confidential message was transmitted. Did it concern someone you know; a friend? A person you think highly of? Your lover, perhaps. Is that why you ran away? Did someone try to make you reveal the fabric of that message?'

It became obvious that they were not going to get any response from the girl in the bed, no matter how they approached her, so Max gave Connie the nod to wind things up. She got to her feet and put the chair back alongside the locker, then smiled at Maria.

'I'll come again when you're feeling better. We'll talk then. Is there anything you'd like me to bring you? Anyone you'd like a visit from? Any message I can give to someone on the base? No?'

Max was already sliding the curtains aside when a quavery voice said, 'I want to come back.'

He turned to see tears on her cheeks. 'No problem there,' he told her. 'As soon as the doctor gives the go ahead you can transfer to the Medical Centre. I'll have a word with him on the way out. It could be tomorrow or the next day.'

'We'll inform Lieutenant Carfax that you'll soon be back,' Connie added. 'Anyone else?'

But that was probing too far. Silence returned and the patient's back was turned.

Returning to the car, having decided Clare was the best person to arrange Norton's transfer to the base, Max thanked Connie for her efforts.

'Head against brick wall. Once she's back with us it'll be easier. What did you deduce from her decision to return despite leaving with all her belongings just three days ago?'

'She's done what he demanded of her with a deal of

violence, so she now expects the affair to take up where it left off.'

He glanced sideways at her as they set off. 'You don't think it was your speech about her singing success and future prospects in that direction, plus the thought of promotion made her see what she would be missing out on?'

Connie shook her head. 'Passion is definitely behind this. She's got rid of the baby he didn't want, and forgiven him for knocking her almost senseless. Now she thinks everything'll be rosy, silly bitch. When she discovers he has no intention of resuming the affair she'll be off again. Just you wait.'

'There speaks the voice of the complete female cynic,' he said with some amusement. 'And you look such a nice, kind person.'

'I am,' she protested laughingly. 'It's this job that makes me cynical.'

By the end of the afternoon they could establish several facts which merely eliminated possibilities. Tom had checked Staff Andrews' story regarding leaving his vehicle for repairs on the forecourt of the Jewish firm in the early hours of Sunday morning. The owners returning late from a party had seen it there. They offered to return it if they could collect what was owing.

'I've also Bill Jensen's evidence of seeing Vince Andrews at the Recreation Centre on the nights they were rehearsing *Carmen*,' he told the team. 'In fact, he had a beer with him on several of those occasions under the impression Staff had been attending one of the classes.'

'You think he's in the clear?' asked Max sharply.

'On what he told me today my gut feeling is that he knew nothing of the attack on Norton, but it clarified evidence we already have.' Throwing Piercey a glowering look, he said, 'That call you interrupted in Norton's dressing room was from Staff Andrews. He said she promised to call him back in ten, which is what you heard her say. When she didn't, he drove to her accommodation block, saw her arrive then jump straight into your Audi which raced up to meet her. The timing fits perfectly.

'He saw the car rocking with what he believed was highly active sex, but was more likely to have been caused by the assault on her.' Glancing back at Max, he said, 'The RMP Post is just three hundred metres from the copse. I suggest Chummy either pushed Norton out where that took place, or he drove to within easy staggering distance of it before dumping her. That would make sense of how Norton managed to reach help in her distressed state.'

'It still doesn't explain why she claimed *I* beat her up,' Piercey complained vigorously.

'Her attacker was driving *your* car,' Tom snapped. 'We have a witness to the fact. Until you produce solid evidence that proves you were elsewhere, you remain the prime suspect.'

Max intervened. 'Staff Andrews reckons he left the Sergeants' Mess to drive to Norton's living quarters, where she came in her own vehicle just five or so minutes later. Comparing the timings we already have with those he offers, Chummy must have taken the Audi from the mess car parking area shortly after Phil left it there, in order to race up and skid to a halt almost as Norton arrived. As Staff Andrews didn't witness the carjacking, we now have very precise timing which ties in with Private Jimmy James' statement concerning what *he* saw that night. I suggest the phone call Norton made moments before she left the theatre was to advise someone that Phil was on his way to the Mess, and that person was there ready to carry out his plan. That young woman surely conspired to set Phil up. Once she's back on base she'll be charged with going AWOL and with giving false information. That's for starters. Hopefully, she'll then realize the mess she's in and decide to cooperate.'

'I wouldn't count on it,' said Connie. 'She's a very determined woman. Add overwhelming passion and you have someone who won't behave in reasonable fashion. She's Carmen. Flamboyant, daring, hot-headed. She'll need watching carefully.'

'The cynic speaking?' teased Max.

Connie indicated her friend Heather. 'We spoke to a number of both men and women in the cast of the opera, and repeatedly heard that Norton practically metamorphosed into the character she played. It's my guess she hasn't yet fully reverted to Corporal Norton, who handles confidential and highly sensitive communications.'

'On that subject, are we still considering the possibility of breached security being behind the attack on her?' asked Beeny.

Tom nodded. 'Until we find indisputable proof of what really went on in the early hours of last Sunday, we continue to consider every scenario.'

'Including the one that has me in the bloody centre of it,' growled Phil Piercey.

'There's no smoke without fire,' Heather murmured.

Tom had clearly had enough. He wrapped up the briefing with the advice that everyone should consider the firm evidence they had and return in the morning with a fresh concept to offer.

'And *you*,' he ended, looking pointedly at Piercey. 'You rack your brains for an incident which instilled in someone the need for revenge of this magnitude. There *has* to be a reason for the assault to take place in your car, and for the victim to name you repeatedly.'

Everyone departed leaving Max with Tom. He took the opportunity to say, 'D'you really believe the foundation of the crime was to take revenge on Phil?'

Tom glanced across from the papers he was lining up. 'Why else set him up as they did?'

'Convenient patsy?'

Tom walked to the safe and deposited the confidential reports, then locked them away. 'There were half a dozen others trying their luck with her. Why pick Phil?'

'As Derek Beeny said, an opportunity to get one in against the law and order lads.'

'Nah, there has to be a more calculated reason than that, and I wager he bloody knows what it is.'

Max regarded him frankly. 'He's one of ours, Tom. Don't malign his integrity. He's a wild card, at times, but he's made of sterling stuff.'

Tom nodded. 'He needs a prod to keep him from getting too sure of himself. He still can't prove he was in his room in the Mess when the assault took place, and evidence is piling up against him.' He perched on the edge of a desk. 'Is there any chance Norton will retract her accusation and name the man who beat her up?'

Max shrugged. 'Connie seems sure the girl is totally mixed up even about her own identity, at the moment. I'll call in at the Medical Centre and get Clare or Duncan MacPherson to contact the hospital about transferring the patient asap. We might have better luck with Norton once she's on home ground.'

'It'll be interesting to discover who contacts or visits her.'

'Or who *doesn't*. Connie reckons the lover will have no intention of resuming the affair even though the baby has been aborted.'

'Makes sense,' Tom agreed, taking up his car keys. 'Something like that puts the kibosh on romance, especially if the bloke's a married man having a fling.'

They began walking from the building. 'Talking of romance, it seems our lady doctor has got herself engaged. Nora saw her this morning wearing a whacking great ring on the appropriate finger. Know who the lucky man is?'

Max grinned. 'Can't keep a secret on this damned base. We'll be inviting you all to our celebration party on Sunday.'

Tom halted and offered his hand. 'Congratulations. Nora reckons you've found the right one, this time, and I agree.'

Learning from MacPherson that Clare had already left the Medical Centre, Max recruited the Scottish doctor's professional assistance to arrange Maria Norton's transfer as soon as the German doctor considered it possible.

'I'd like her installed in a single room. That one at the far end of the corridor will be ideal. She'll technically be under arrest on at least two counts, so I'll arrange twenty-four-hour surveillance outside her door.'

'No, you will not,' MacPherson returned smartly. 'This is

my domain. *I* give the orders. Any decisions concerning patients in my care are *mine*. This woman you want to transfer here will become one of them and, as such, you'll have no authority over her while she remains in this building.' His eyes were bright with anger, reflecting the fabled quick temper of redheads. 'I'll no tolerate any *guards* sitting outside my wards.'

Getting into his stride, he said, 'The lass is a *victim*, man. She was brutally assaulted by one of your detectives, then underwent a crude abortion which could well have so damaged her she'll never reproduce. No, you certainly will not treat her as a prisoner in my hospital.'

Trying to keep his patience in the face of this tirade, Max said tautly, 'I'm not suggesting handcuffing her to the bloody bed! I simply want a discreet watch kept on her.'

'I've said no.'

'Then I'll post uniformed guards *outside* your domain. I have full authority to do that and it'll be anything but discreet.'

They stood in the small consulting room facing each other aggressively: two big men testing each other's staying power. If there was an underlying element of lingering sexual rivalry Max chose not to recognize it.

Eventually, MacPherson said, 'That would be way over the top. Talk sense.'

'Fair enough.' Max took a deep breath to give himself time to find the best words. 'Yes, Maria Norton was a victim of assault. Just one day later she left your domain, collected all her belongings, and absconded taking every precaution against being traced. That was her own decision. Seeking a backstreet abortionist was also her sole decision. When a female colleague and I visited her today she refused to speak to us. She neither answered our questions nor accepted our offers of help. Only as we were leaving did she say, "I want to come back." Hence why I'm here.'

'And I've agreed to arrange her transfer, but I see no reason to treat her as a prisoner.'

'But *I* do,' Max insisted. 'I'm a policeman. I deal with lawbreakers, and this woman has broken several. She went absent without leave giving the impression that she didn't mean to return; she gave a statement describing the assault on her person which we have proved to be a pack of lies, and we have evidence to suggest that she conspired with someone to accuse an innocent man of the brutal attack on her. Yes, she was a victim, but our inquiries point to her being a victim of her own criminal machinations.'

After a moment of reflection MacPherson said, 'So what do you imagine she might do while in my charge?'

'Ah, now it's your turn to talk sense. And, by the way, you're not the only person qualified to make a decision on this. Clare treated Norton when she was first brought in. Her opinion must be sought.'

'Oh aye, be sure to consult her. I shall still object to having policemen sitting outside my wards. The poor woman will be quite unfit to run amok through this building.'

Max gave a heavy sigh. 'Let's drop the question until Norton arrives here. You'll then see the frame of mind she's in and understand why I think it essential to keep her under observation. It's my impression she's in a volatile mental state. While I don't expect her to consider killing herself, I've no hesitation in reading into her desire to return the expectation of resuming her relationship with the man who fathered the baby. Experience tells me that's very unlikely. When she discovers that, there's a chance she might harm herself. Or even abscond again.

'There's also a third possibility. She could have been attacked because she was privy to highly sensitive information transmitted while she was on duty. If that was so, she could be under further threat once she's back on the base.'

He prepared to depart leaving the matter unresolved for the moment. He had had enough of MacPherson's attitude for now. Time to resume hostilities when the sick corporal was acutally here in the ward.

'We not only bang-up soldiers who break the law, we aim to protect them from reprisals.' He stopped in the doorway and looked back. 'We also pledge to prove the innocence of those wrongly accused. In this instance it's one of my own team. I defend his rights as strongly as you defend yours, Duncan.'

The hospital doctors wanted to keep Maria Norton for at least five more days to allow time for counselling sessions. Max and Clare had exchanged words on the subject of police personnel on chairs outside wards, she supporting MacPherson's views, so news of a delay in the patient's return was timely. They let the matter drop.

The next day being a Friday when it was usual for everything to wind down early, there was additional reason for normal activities to cease by mid-afternoon. The band of the Drumdorran Fusiliers was to give a marching display to officially welcome the West Wiltshire Regiment back from Afghanistan, and to impress Top Brass who had arrived for tactical discussions with the returning commanders. This stirring display would end with Beating the Retreat, after which personnel could buy hot food and drinks from stalls set up around the parade ground.

In view of this, Max agreed with Tom that they could make little advance on the Norton case until the start of the next week. After hearing any fresh reflections the team might have, which were few, the team completed overdue reports on several minor cases they had been dealing with before leaving with promises to attend Max and Clare's party on Sunday evening.

For the first time since they had both moved into the matching apartments the large connecting room was fully used. As well as members of 26 Section, Major MacPherson and senior medical staff had been invited. The hosts employed the caterers Clare had found while Max was in Spain, and the large table bore an impressive selection of the company's festive fare.

It was a very merry occasion. Any personality clashes were put aside, and when someone began playing popular tunes on

Clare's piano an impromptu sing-song began. So fully did guests participate it was a while before Max grew aware of the landline telephone ringing. He took the call with some misgivings. Who could be contacting them at this hour? There were no immediate neighbours to complain of noise, and all their friends and colleagues were here.

'Max Rydal,' he said above the vigorous singing.

'George Maddox, sir. Sorry to interrupt your Sunday but I gather Major MacPherson is with you at the moment. We need a doctor urgently. We have a serious ongoing situation.'

Max's heart sank. 'He'll be on the way asap. Give me a few details, George,' he said taking the phone through to the relative quiet of his own apartment.

'It's another violent assault, this time on the ADC of one of the visiting staff officers. Sarn't Pocock found him on the road bordering the copse and called an ambulance. He's at the Medical Centre receiving treatment, but a doctor should be present. It's a worse battering than Norton's and I think SIB should be in on this.'

'Yes. I'll send Tom Black.'

Disconnecting, Max threaded his way between the cluster of guests to reach Duncan MacPherson, who was deep in conversation with Olly Simpson.

'Duty calls, Duncan,' he said, drawing the man aside to give the details. 'Why do these calls always come when we're having fun?'

'It was ever thus, Max. Give my thanks to your future wife for a most enjoyable evening . . . until now. Goodnight. I'll let myself out.'

Catching sight of Tom looking inquisitively at the departing Scot, Max motioned to his friend to go with him into his apartment. He came very smartly, his policeman's instinct working overtime.

'Norton done another runner?' he asked.

Max shook his head. 'We have a second ABH. One of the visiting ADCs has been found on the road by the copse having been thoroughly done over. George said it's worse than the attack on Norton. One of George's squad will be at the Medical Centre, but this is another case for us.'

'I'll get going.' Tom headed for Max's personal front door, and he followed.

'Same method, same location, same day of the week. Have we been up a gum tree, Tom? This can't have anything to do with an opera and a girl who thinks she's Carmen. Do we actually have a serial sadist on our hands?'

NINE

On Monday morning Max followed Clare to the Medical Centre in the hope of interviewing Captain Rory Smythe. Tom had contacted Max in the early hours to say the ADC was too traumatized to speak. They now found nothing had changed overnight, so Clare promised to call Max once the officer had recovered sufficiently to be interviewed.

At Headquarters the ennui over the stalemate in the Norton case had been banished by this new dramatic attack. Before Tom began the general briefing Max had a short discussion with him on what they had gleaned about the victim from his military record, which they had both checked out. Smythe had been rated a diligent and generally proficient cadet at Sandhurst, who was then commissioned into the West Wiltshire Regiment where he served until two years ago when he became ADC to Major-General Bishop.

Max said, 'I suspect our victim had friends in the right places, Tom. He was no more than an average cadet at Sandhurst. He's now thirty-six and there's no mention of distinction in the field, either in Iraq or Afghanistan.'

'Or mention of useful skills like foreign languages, in-depth personal knowledge of Middle Eastern countries, or a special proficiency in any aspect of battle strategy.'

'Exactly. So he's a better administrator than a warrior, which is why his usefulness as an ADC has been recruited. He must have a quick brain or he wouldn't have held the post for two years. You saw him last night. Is he a big man? Would it take two to beat him up?'

Tom shook his head. 'Couldn't see much of his frame. Thin and wiry, I'd guess. If he was jumped in the darkness, one hefty blow could have stunned him enough to enable the attacker to do quite a lot of damage without resistance from his victim.'

'As ever, the big question is why. On the surface he appears to be a solid dependable assistant to his senior officer, with no special flair for or insight to specialist info he could be cowed by force into revealing.'

'In other words, are the two attacks linked in some way, or totally coincidental? Has Captain Smythe some connection with Maria Norton?'

Max nodded at his office door to indicate that they should join the team, saying as he walked, 'Norton must be interviewed more determinedly, and I'll arrange to speak to Major-General Bishop when there's an opportunity. I doubt he'll be able to throw much light on the case, but I'd like the man's assessment of his Aide.'

There was immediate silence when they appeared, Piercey looking particularly alert. They had all learned the basics of what had occurred before leaving the party last night, where Piercey had instantly pointed out that he had a foolproof alibi this time.

'Captain Smythe is still too ill to be interviewed,' Tom began, 'so we have very little info to start with. I spoke to Sergeant Pocock last night and all he could tell me was that he spotted a body at the side of the road near where the main track through the copse begins. Thinking it strange that his mates would have abandoned someone out there, and having his wife in the car, he pulled up just beyond the still figure and approached with caution. It was soon apparent the man was not drunk or high on drugs, but that he had been quite viciously attacked.

'There's no question of Sarn't Pocock being responsible. He and his wife had celebrated their wedding anniversary in town with two other couples and were heading home. He denies seeing anyone near or moving about in the copse. Nor did he pass any other cars along that stretch of the perimeter road. It was one of those times when there was little traffic returning to the base.

'Until the doctors have fully examined the victim we won't know whether there are signs that he was pushed from a vehicle after the attack, and until George's boys have completed a search of the area there's no evidence that it happened at the spot where he was found. Or even in that vicinity. What we can do is discuss the possibility of there being a common denominator in the two cases.'

'Or eliminate it,' Max added. 'Last night I read too much into the similarity of method, location and day of the week. On reflection I found much to dispute that hasty conclusion. Your input, please.'

To no one's surprise Piercey pointed out that no way could he be a suspect. 'Norton was seen jumping eagerly into my Audi, then being driven to the copse where the rocking of the car suggested hectic sex. Maybe it was, and the assault came later, but there was an indisputable intention to involve me in whatever was going down that night. This *must* be a separate case.'

Beeny agreed with his friend. 'Ask the Uniforms. They deal with punch-ups, general aggression, impromptu fights all the time, but they don't imagine deep plots to link them together.'

Max's lips twitched with amusement. 'You think I'm off on a mystery story, do you?'

Beeny smiled. 'One of your wild geese, perhaps.'

'There is one possible link,' offered Olly Simpson in his usual laconic fashion.

'Let's have it,' urged Tom, clearly irritated by Piercey's second attempt to justify his innocence.

'Norton has access to classified info, which Smythe might also have.'

'And Norton's Troop Commander is concerned about a communication Maria received before she was attacked last week,' added Heather. 'Could both victims have been privy to secret knowledge someone's desperate to learn?'

Piercey was still on the defence. 'If he was that desperate, why wait a week before attacking a different victim? He'd have had a second go at Maria before this. I say they're different cases.'

'So we return to Captain Goodey's nutshell theory regarding Norton and continue our search for the father of the aborted foetus while we try to untangle this second puzzle. As to the first, the holder of the key to it is Norton herself,' Tom said somewhat unnecessarily. 'She resisted Connie's gentle persuasion, so I want you to take a tougher line with her, Heather. The doctor on her case wants her to have several counselling sessions to ease her confusion. Be sympathetic and get her talking. Be the friend she doesn't apparently have. You're one of a large family; you know how to gain people's confidence. Once you have hers make her aware of how she could minimize the trouble she's in.'

Max intervened to point out that Heather might have some opposition from hospital staff. 'If so, do get across to them that we need to trace and punish whoever forced her with violence to take the risk of an amateur abortion.' He smiled ruefully. 'It might turn into a long, boring wait, but insist on being allowed to talk to her. What happened last night makes it imperative.'

Heather nodded. 'She can't keep it up forever. It's natural for a woman to unburden herself after something like that. Hopefully, she'll prefer to confide in me rather than a German counsellor.'

Tom pushed on. 'Now the new case. Captain Smythe is a former member of the West Wilts. I'll interview him when I'm given the go-ahead, but I want the rest of you to check for regimental members presently on base who could have served with him two or more years ago. Go and talk to them. Get a description of what he was like as a regimental commander, and any info on incidents concerning him which could have a bearing on this attack. His service record shows he was divorced three years ago. Get the gen on that and any opinions on why he left the regiment to take on his present job. Was he tactically moved sideways, or did he go at his own request? OK, get going. Call in with any vital disclosures, as usual. Also, as usual, keep eyes and ears open for anything on the Norton case. It isn't in limbo while we follow up on the second victim.'

*   *   *

Max called Headquarter Company to discover when Major-General Bishop might be available to speak to him, and was told that the visiting officers were scheduled to take a break at eleven hundred for coffee. Deciding that it would be in the Officers' Mess used by Headquarters staff and officers who were not transitory, Max drove across the base shortly before eleven and asked the Mess Sergeant to pass a message to Bishop when he arrived and deposited his cap on the table used for the purpose in the foyer.

Shortly after the group entered, Max was approached and told the General would be happy to speak to him about Captain Smythe's unfortunate accident. Walking to the anteroom Max thought caustically that men of Bishop's calibre had a way of dismissing even the most serious disasters as things that simply could not be helped. He supposed that came under the heading of keeping calm and in control of the situation; instructions for commanders of men in battle.

Major-General Bishop was a tall man with flaxen hair and rather piercing blue eyes, who was in conversation with a West Wilts captain Max knew well.

Approaching, Max said, 'Thank you for giving me some time, sir.' Then he added, 'Hallo, it's good to see you safely back,' to Guy Strand, who returned the greeting with a smile before stepping away with his coffee cup to allow the other two to talk privately.

'Your people acted very promptly, I hear,' said Bishop, walking towards a quiet corner of the large room with Max.

'We'll know more when Captain Smythe is able to tell us what happened, sir. There was no abandoned vehicle in the vicinity and it seems unlikely that he would have been walking near the copse at that hour. We believe he was either taken there after the assault, or went willingly with someone who unexpectedly became violent and abandoned him there. We'll know more by the end of the day,' he added with confidence. 'What I'd like from you is some personal knowledge concerning your ADC. He served with the West Wiltshire Regiment until two years ago. I understand you are here for discussions with the commanders of the troops just returned from Afghanistan, so Captain Smythe might well meet some former colleagues on base. Did he mention it, say he was hoping to reunite with an old friend or two?'

The older man's brow furrowed. 'We're under way with five days of in-depth technical investigation and planning, Captain Rydal, which often continues until late in the evening. Then there are the reports of the day's findings to write. I'm afraid I've had little time to talk to Rory about anything but the day's events, and on his part he wouldn't attempt to discuss his personal plans with me.'

He put his empty coffee cup on the window sill. 'He's the best ADC I've had because, like me, he concentrates on doing his job well and never muddies the water with inconsequential chatter about his private life. We're not *chums*, we're a bloody good team.'

Max understood him. Master and servant. Once the distance between them narrows too far it can reduce the effectiveness of them both. In the armed forces that can prove to be dangerous. Max could not help wondering if Smythe acted the punctilious servant for his own advantage. Why did he transfer from a fighting unit? Had he something to hide?

Knowing he was not going to get much useful information from this hardened leader of men, Max said somewhat superfluously, 'So you have no input on who might have attacked Captain Smythe, or why?'

'None whatsoever. As far as I was aware, he was compiling reports on what had been discussed and formulated during the day's conference, as he did every evening.'

'Well, thank you, sir. As soon as we have anything substantial to report you'll be informed.'

He turned away and was so lost in musing on the lack of interest in Rory Smythe as a person rather than a robotic subordinate, he would have brushed past another group if someone had not hailed him. He stopped and glanced round to see a tall, good-looking man with dark waving hair and lively green eyes studying him closely. Andrew Rydal had always been a striking man; his recent second marriage had enhanced his attraction.

'Hallo, sir. I wasn't aware that you were here for the conference,' Max said rather coolly.

His father moved away from the group. 'I'm not. Just passing through and using the base as a handy B and B.' He offered his hand. 'It's good to see you back on your feet and on the job. So the medics have given you A1 status again.'

'No, that's still ahead. I'm just acting as general dogsbody. We've two complex cases on hand . . .'

'And you can't resist joining in,' Andrew finished with a smile. 'You always liked to be in the thick of things.'

Max was amazed. He was not aware that his father had taken that much interest in him. 'Something like that.'

'Bad business about Rory Smythe.'

They had moved to a corner near the double doors, out of the hearing of even the closest group. Max did not believe the excuse about using the base as a B and B. Brigadier Rydal was a member of the Joint Intelligence Committee and as such moved around the world on covert business. He was never 'just passing through' without some solid reason for being there. And he had deliberately brought up the name of the battered ADC. Max pursued that line.

'He's still under sedation so we've been unable to question him. We'll know a lot more by tonight. Do you know him?'

'Mmm, by repute,' came the casual response. 'An excellent admin bod, apparently.'

'General Bishop thinks so, but he appears to have little interest in him as a person.'

Andrew gave a faint smile. 'Billy Bishop's a stickler for rank. He'll defend his men fiercely and succour the wounded, but he never makes friends of them. Descends from a long line of distinguished generals who were deeply respected but never loved by their troops.'

Max was surprised by this comment. He had never known his father to speak so frankly about other serving officers. Actually, they met so infrequently the threads of their lives were too loosely entwined for conversation to be anything but hesitant and rather stilted.

On impulse he asked, 'How did your men regard you, d'you think?'

Andrew's eyebrows rose at the unexpected question, and he dealt with it by saying smoothly, 'I was never beaten up and left by the side of a road.' Then, equally smoothly, he threw something unexpected at Max. 'Congratulations are in order, I believe.'

'Er . . . yes. How did you . . . ?'

'Major MacPherson gave out the news. I met Clare at the hospital last November. You weren't in a fit state to register much of what was going on around you, but I thought then that there were the makings of a good relationship between you two. I'm glad it's worked out so well.' He began moving away. 'Send us an invitation to the wedding. I can't guarantee my own attendance, but Helene will want to be there. She adores bridal ceremonies.' Looking back as he made to rejoin the group he had been with, he said lightly, 'Keep away from stressed men with explosives in future.'

It took Max several moments to get his thoughts back on track after that, and they were still muddled when he spotted Livya in conversation with a major in the opposite corner. Her gaze held his for a long while before she made signs of approaching him. Max avoided that by giving a slight nod of acknowledgement and leaving the anteroom swiftly. Of course she would be with Andrew wherever he went on military duty. Continuing the agony of unrequited love! Well, that was her decision.

Outside in his car, Max put aside the folly of the woman he had believed he loved last year and reviewed the short interlude with his father. What was he really doing here? More to the point, how had he encountered Duncan MacPherson to learn of the engagement? He sat for some minutes piecing together the salient points in that brief conversation, arriving at an ambiguous conclusion.

Andrew had swiftly introduced the subject of Rory

Smythe. Max now saw it as deliberate in order to discover if SIB had learned anything from the assault victim. Had Andrew tried to interview Smythe and been forestalled by the Scottish doctor who had strict rules, no matter who he was dealing with? And what about the comment that he had never been beaten up and left by the side of a road, followed very swiftly by a total change of subject? Was this member of the Joint Intelligence Committee rather too interested in an ordinary ADC?

Shortly before noon Clare called Max to say Rory Smythe had fully emerged from sedation and could be interviewed. Max passed the news to Tom, not necessarily as a sign of acceptance that his deputy was officially commanding 26 Section, but more because he, himself, had discovered a wild goose he was keen to pursue. The WG in this case was Guy Strand who, unfortunately, was very involved in the conference which would not be over until late tomorrow.

However, Guy was an interviewee, not an investigator who needed to write up reports each evening, so Max drove back to the Mess where lunch would certainly be eaten by those who had drunk coffee there earlier and sat in his car watching for them to return.

When they appeared in twos and threes, deep in conversation, Max noted the absence of his father and Livya with satisfaction. Oh yes, Brigadier Rydal was following a trail of his own. And his son had a good idea of what it was. Giving Guy ten minutes to make use of the cloakroom and order himself a drink at the bar, Max called the man's mobile.

'Captain Strand.'

'Max Rydal. Couldn't stay to talk during the coffee break and I know you're tied up with this conference all day, so how about meeting in our own Mess around eighteen hundred?'

'Today?'

'If you're free. Last time we met you told me you'd got engaged. I've just taken that same step. How about a celebratory drink?'

'Er . . . fine! It'll be good to get away from the Top Brass and relax. I'll call if there's any change of plan.'

'Likewise.'

Guy had been unable to hide his surprise. They had met up on purely military business on many occasions, but were not normally drinking buddies. Max liked the young man who had developed into an excellent officer during the period they had known each other, collecting a commendation for rescuing a colleague under fire, but the intention was to meet Guy tonight for a more serious reason than an exchange of felicitations.

Rory Smythe was still looking dazed. His eyes were glassy and lifeless, his gaze somewhat vacant, his face and neck a mass of bruises. His right arm from elbow to wrist was in plaster; both hands were encased in soft medical mittens.

Taking all this in Tom had no doubt the rest of the man's body had suffered equally badly. No impromptu drunken brawl this. It had been premeditated punishment possibly by more than one person. This victim had created strong, uncontrollable anger somewhere along his way, and had suffered the consequences last night.

Tom approached the bed. 'Sarn't Major Black, SIB, sir. Captain Goodey thinks you're up to answering a few questions now. The sooner we learn the details of what happened the sooner we can arrest who was responsible. In your own time, sir.'

Smythe's gaze remained blank. It was as if he saw right through Tom and was deaf to his voice.

'Captain Smythe, we need to know who attacked you and where the assault took place. Was it carried out by more than one person? Did you recognize anyone? Did they say anything to you? Have you any idea who might have been responsible?'

Nothing.

'Sir, we can't begin to bring the perpetrators to justice unless you tell us about the events of last night which led to your being violently attacked. Why were you in that unlit area of the perimeter road on foot? Were you taken there? Had you arranged to meet someone?'

Again nothing. Tom began to lose patience.

'We know there was no abandoned car in the vicinity to suggest your voluntary presence, so were you jumped elsewhere then taken to the copse?'

Still silence.

'Captain Smythe, you're doing yourself no favours with this attitude,' snapped Tom. 'A serious crime has been committed against you and it's SIB's responsibility to bring to justice whoever was responsible. Please answer my questions.'

The slightest movement of the mittened hands, a blink of the staring eyes, a tongue running over swollen lips, then a faint voice saying, 'A nasty bang on the head. I remember nothing. Absolutely nothing. Sorry.'

Heather Johnson was having no more luck than Tom. After waiting for three hours to speak to Maria Norton she was told the patient was very upset after the counselling session and would need to recover during a period of solitary reflection. Perhaps the police lady would like to have something to eat in the café and return in an hour or so.

When she did, Heather was barred from the ward because the patient was in an induced sleep. Not all the energetic explanations of the need to apprehend a serious criminal made the medical staff relax their stance. At sixteen thirty she called Tom's number to report failure.

'I can't storm in there, sir,' she said wearily. 'I don't think I'm going to get anywhere with this today. All right if I try again in the morning?'

'Yes, yes. Don't, for God's sake, stay there all night. It's obviously a general no-go day today. I've cancelled a briefing until the morning, so go home and drown your sorrows as I plan to do.'

Max was in the middle of filling in a veritable pile of forms in advance of his appearance before a medical board, which had arrived that morning, and was cursing the invasiveness of the questions, when Tom poked his head around the office door to announce that he had finished business for the day and was off home.

'I sometimes wish Nora would give *me* a bang on the head so I could conveniently forget things I'd rather not remember.'

Max smiled. 'Norton's bound to crack eventually. She said she wants to get back here – presumably to reunite with her lover – so perhaps that's the requisite carrot. We'll offer it tomorrow. As for Sonny Smythe, I have hopes of finding another way in to that particular mystery. See you tomorrow, Tom. Regards to Nora and the family. You're a lucky man, d'you know that?'

'Yes. Once you get spliced you can start rearing your own.'

Max nodded happily. 'That's the idea. Goodnight.'

For a few minutes after Tom's departure Max ignored his boring task and allowed himself to dream up a future family. Maybe he and Clare should start the process now. Why wait for the marriage service?

His landline rang to fragment the dream, but when he heard Clare's voice he started to put it together again. Then he registered the urgency in her tone.

'Something wrong?' he asked.

'You'll be the better judge of that. Captain Smythe has just been driven away in an ambulance, destination unknown. The attendants had a genuine document of transfer, signed and stamped. Both Duncan and I questioned the move, and he rang for official confirmation before allowing it to take place because we normally have advance notification of transfers. Duncan was given a brusque affirmative, nothing more. Your victim has been spirited away, Max.'

TEN

Deep in thought, Max left the Medical Centre to drive to his meeting with Guy Strand. Both Clare and Duncan had been vocal about the peremptory manner in which Rory Smythe had been taken from their care. Regulations had been ignored, although higher authority had rubber-stamped it.

Max shared their resentment. Am I overreacting? he asked himself. I should be glad to have the investigation taken off our hands while we're still grappling with the complex Norton case, yet there is something here which smacks of intrigue. I need to be totally satisfied that there is no link between the two assaults.

Guy arrived late, apologizing and shaking Max's hand warmly. 'Heard about the explosives in a garden shed. It's good to see you up and about, looking pretty well all in one piece.' He walked towards the bar. 'Let's get a round in fast. I thought we'd never shake off the Brass. Such nit-pickers! It can't be that long ago they were in combat. Falklands, Bosnia, Kosovo, Iraq twice, and this ten-year war we're still fighting – they must have been involved in one of those – yet they drone on and on about the minor details you don't have time for when you're eyeball to eyeball with the enemy.' He rapped his knuckles on the bar counter to attract the steward's attention. 'Ah, well! What'll you have, Max?'

They settled with their beer in two easy chairs in a quiet corner, and Guy immediately embarked on the subject he believed they had met to celebrate. His mobile features, deeply browned by the Afghan climate, still bore signs of strain resulting from six months of warfare, his large hand holding the glass had a slight tremor, and he spoke in the rapid clipped tones of men used to giving orders.

'*So*, you're also taking the plunge into matrimony.'

'That's right. We're thinking of September. How about you? Now you're home you can get down to making plans, I suppose.'

Guy grinned. 'She did all that while I was away. Had the dress made by Nora Black, booked the church, sent out invitations. For Saturday week.'

The conversation continued along those lines for some minutes before Max broached the subject he really wanted to discuss. 'So the meetings with the aforesaid nit-pickers today had one bod missing. Have they supplied General Bishop with a replacement?'

'Not that I noticed. Tell the truth, I have other things on my mind and these long drawn-out sessions are getting me down. Why don't the buggers go out there to get the info first-hand instead of arranging conferences that keep us from starting our well-earned leave?'

'Always a rhetorical question, Guy.' Max offered a second beer, and when he returned with them said, 'Rory Smythe was formerly with the West Wilts, wasn't he? Did you ever come across him while he was with the regiment?'

Guy took a long drink from his glass, then shook his head. 'Six months without alcohol makes a man eager to compensate. You were saying?'

'Did you ever serve alongside Rory Smythe?'

'Oh, you know how it is. You cross the path of hundreds in your time, some of them more than once.'

'And Smythe?' prompted Max.

Another long draught of beer. 'Well, it was a while ago. Couple of years or more.' He frowned. 'That's right. My second deployment to Afghanistan. I'd had a six-month detachment to 23 Regiment. Had grand ideas of joining the SAS.' He pulled a face. 'Didn't make the grade. Failed the last hurdle and somewhat ignominiously returned to a different battalion which was scheduled for a stint in the war zone. Those SAS blokes are tougher than tough. My God, you wouldn't believe . . .'

'And Rory Smythe was in the battalion you joined, was he?' Max asked swiftly, fearing his companion was straying from the subject.

'Oh . . . yes. Didn't have much to do with him. You don't unless you indulge in the same off-duty pastimes. I'm a sport and fitness freak. He's more the intellectual type. Bumped up against him in the Mess, that's all.'

Guy suddenly caught on to why Max was interested in Smythe. 'Of course, you're landed with finding who beat him up, and why. Can't help you there. Only returned to base five days ago. Besides, after he took the ADC post I never saw him again. Until now.'

'Did he speak to you?'

Guy gave a sour smile. 'Just a stiff nod of recognition. Too high and mighty to be chummy with fighting soldiers. Must say he appears to be better equipped for the task of general dogsbody to a general.'

'You didn't rate him very high as a company commander?'

A glance at his watch suggested Guy was preparing to wind up the meeting. 'As I said, I didn't spend off-duty time with him, but one hears things during the claustrophobic conditions of combat.'

'Such as?'

'He wasn't popular with the rank and file. The NCOs virtually ran the company and kept morale high in the face of Smythe's ragged control.'

'Ragged control? That's a curious description.'

The other man shrugged. 'Just gossip. You know how it is in all-male situations.'

'Gossip about Smythe?'

Glancing again at his watch, Guy said, 'To be precise, Smythe had his favourites and those he was habitually hard on.'

Max took that up before the subject could be dropped. 'Favourites? D'you mean what I think you mean?'

'As I said, it was just gossip around a camp fire out on patrol. Sex-starved guys getting stimulated to liven up a cold night way out in the endless desert. No proof.' He drained his glass with relish and returned it to the table. 'Mind you,' he added thoughtfully, 'there was a rather strange incident just a week before our stint ended.'

'Oh?'

'Ye – es,' said Guy, remembering. 'One of his platoons was on a night recce and a young lad who'd been with the West Wilts just six months, lost contact with the rest of the patrol. That's highly dangerous. A man can wander forever in the darkness with no way of finding the others. Worse still, he can walk into the enemy camp before he's aware of their presence.'

'And this youngster did?'

Guy wagged his head. 'The way I heard it, the corporal leading the patrol halted them soon as they discovered he was missing, and almost immediately they heard a shot no more than fifty or so metres away.'

'And?'

'That was the strange part. They took up defensive positions, but silence reigned. Once the corporal judged the situation to be stable he had his patrol ready to give him cover while he crawled out towards the sound of the single shot. We never leave our wounded or dead, no matter how tricky it is to retrieve them, as you know.'

'Did he find the casualty?'

'So I heard. Shot in the head. No sign of the enemy.' He frowned, visions returning of the conflict he had left just a week ago. 'Not uncommon, that. They take advantage of a perfect target then melt away before the entire patrol can catch them.' He drew in a deep breath. 'They're happy to pick off one or two at a time, then retire from retaliation. They have eternity lying before them, Max, knowing we'll call it a day eventually. Then they'll have their barren but awesomely beautiful land to themselves again.'

His gaze seemingly into that distant country must have refocussed on the clock above the bar. 'Christ!' he ejaculated, getting to his feet. 'I'm due to meet Pam to discuss the order of service for the wedding with the Padre. Daren't be late. She'd kill me.'

Max also stood and smiled. 'Bad start to a marriage partnership, and I'd have another case to investigate. Good luck, Guy.'

'And thanks,' he added silently as he watched the man walk from the bar. 'You've just given me a very interesting scenario to work on.'

Phil Piercey was deeply depressed once more. A call to Heather had revealed that she had made no progress on her attempt to break Maria's silence. In fact, she had been unable even to see her. Until that lying bitch withdrew her allegation the charge against him would stand, despite solid evidence that most of her account of the events on that Saturday night was false. Nothing would erase the accusation against him, but he needed official notification of his innocence of any involvement.

Additional cause for his depression was this new case which threatened to shelve the other one so frustratingly static. A general's ADC. Yeah, of course that would push aside the roughing-up of a half-Spanish singing corporal, he thought sourly as he sat in his Audi in the darkness gazing at the copse.

He could understand why this was a good location for a crime. An Anglo-Russian major had been shot here three years ago and his body hung on a post outside the Officers' Mess. Well away from any building, this stretch of road had a number of bends. It was the perfect spot for . . . His thoughts were interrupted by guilty recollection of his mad moment with Maria's mobile. If Tom Black ever learned about that it would give him the perfect excuse to kick him out of 26 Section. Out of SIB completely.

He sighed deeply and headed for his room. He was resenting the restrictions on his life more and more. Eight days confined to barracks! He had only been allowed to attend the engagement party because he had travelled with Beeny and Olly Simpson. Two guards! He scowled. Wonder he had not been handcuffed to one of them.

He was still scowling as he parked in his usual spot outside
the Mess. Another solitary evening with DVDs and a six-pack.
He was in no mood for darts, snooker, cards or any other
communal activity. His incarceration could go on for weeks
while full attention was now concentrated on some commissioned general's gofer.

As he left his vehicle he heard a voice shouting, 'Sarge,
Sarge, hang on a minute.'

Looking across at the facing accommodation block he
scowled further at the sight of Private Jimmy James hurrying
towards him. What did the twit want – to measure him for a
suit?

'I've been watching for you,' the storeman panted. 'You're
with the Redcaps, aren't you?'

Piercey could not be bothered to reply, just stood waiting
impatiently for whatever nonsense the man would produce.

'I've seen it.'

'Seen what?' he snapped.

With his round face flushed with excitement, he stumbled
over his next words. 'Just now. I mean, it's there again. Like
it was before. It's . . . *it*.'

'What the hell are you rambling on about? I've better things
to do than listen to a load of crap from you.'

'The *car*. It's there now,' came the triumphant announce-
ment. 'I recognized it straight off, Sarge. Come with me,' he
urged, starting to trot in the direction of the gymnasium.

What James was saying started to make some sense, yet
Piercey was still sceptical as he hesitantly began to follow. 'You
couldn't swear to the colour or make. Even the shape of it.'

'This is it,' James repeated triumphantly. 'I recognized it
straight off, like I told you.'

'How?'

'I'll show you how. Come on, it might go any time.'

'Did you note down the reg number?' demanded Piercey
as they hurried beside the long side wall of the large building.

'Why'd I do that?'

'Oh, for Christ's sake! If this is a . . .' Piercey broke off as they rounded the corner to where a number of vehicles were parked and James went directly to a bronze hatchback and put his hand on it, smiling broadly.

Piercey was disgusted. 'You said it was red. I spent half a day checking red ones out.'

'But it was dark the first time, but soon as I saw *that* I knew it was the same one.' The sticker on the window that he indicated read: BURGESS AND CRABBE QUALITY VEHICLES. 'Such a coincidence,' gushed the storeman. 'Same name as the gentlemen's outfitters I worked for. First time I saw it I thought what a coincidence.'

Holding back a rush of anticipation Piercey glared at the upturned moon face. 'Why the hell didn't you mention this when you were first questioned?'

'Nobody asked about where it was bought. Colour and make was all . . .'

'Bloody idiot!' cried Piercey. 'I could charge you with withholding vital evidence from the police.'

'But nobody *asked* . . .'

He was too busy noting the registration details, which were all he needed to trace the owner. It was just a vehicle seen in the same place on two occasions, no more, but on one of them a serious assault had taken place for which he had been wrongly blamed. A swift glance inside the building revealed that several vigorous games of handball were in progress, but Piercey recalled that Maria had used one of the instructor's offices for vocal exercising on occasion. Had her amorous sessions also taken place here?

He walked pensively back to the hatchback. Chummy parks it here and waits for Maria to tell him his mark is on his way. From the corner of the gymnasium there is a clear view of the Sergeants' Mess. The Audi arrives. The driver (himself) rushes inside carelessly leaving the doors unlocked, and Chummy steals it to drive himself to the assignation with his lover outside her accommodation block. Under the furious gaze of Staff Sergeant Andrews, who is hoping for a reconciliation with Maria, the Audi screeches to a halt and she jumps in with great eagerness before it races off to the lonely area near the copse. Chummy then attacks and abandons her before returning the Audi now containing Maria's gaudy mobile to its original parking spot. Yes. *Yes!* That *was* how it happened!

Running back to the Mess, he did not notice or care where Jimmy James was. The imperative was to check ownership of that hatchback. Now calm and professionally motivated, Piercey scanned the screen then leaned back to stare at the name highlighted there as memory of an incident he had dismissed as unimportant returned.

Next minute he left his room and the building in as big a hurry as he had entered, and sprinted back to the gymnasium. Rounding the corner his pulse raced to see the bronze hatch-back still there. Taking a moment or two to steady himself, he pushed open the double doors and walked through to where one game was still in progress. The players from the other two were clustered at the far end, towels round their necks, drinking from sports flasks as they discussed aspects of their play.

Piercey knew some of them having often enjoyed hard fought but friendly participation in that particular sport. He mingled with them quite casually and joined in their comments and general banter, which suggested he had been observing some of the activity. They were all then drawn to turn and watch the closing stages of a noisy, fast and furious contest which ended with two players flat on their backs claiming they were too exhausted to move.

This, of course, was the spur for others to make sure they did, and during the macho mêlée Piercey made his way from the huge hall unnoticed and jubilant, clutching his trophy. Back in his room he dropped it in an evidence bag and sealed it, then sat gazing at it while he fought an inner battle. His maverick personality yearned to follow through with what he had learned, then present the solution to the case and earn all the kudos. Oh, *how* he longed to do that.

A period of sane and sensible thinking showed him the error of going it alone this time. There was too much at stake. His innocence. The striking from his record of Norton's charge of ABH. And, much as it went against the grain, by following rules and procedures to the letter it would raise his credit with Tom Black and ensure he remained with 26 Section.

When Tom arrived at Headquarters he did not feel particularly optimistic after being told by Max last night that the case concerning the visiting ADC had been taken out of their jurisdiction. Tom was in two minds about that. It certainly halved their present load, but as the assault had taken place on their patch he did not welcome the prospect of SIB from the UK descending on them and flexing their muscles.

Max had sounded very laid back, and that worried Tom. It was not like his friend to accept highhandedness so calmly. Not only highhandedness, but professional discourtesy in removing Smythe without informing 26 Section. Where was he being taken, and why?

Max had contacted their Regional Commander. All Keith Pinkney had been told was that the relevant paperwork was on its way. And Max had left it at that! Oh yes, Tom was worried. If ever there was a wild goose this was one, and Max would surely pursue it. Over the past few days the fact that he was not yet officially back in command had been forgotten. Tom now remembered and called his team to order to give them the news that the second assault would be investigated by someone else.

'But it took place here,' objected Beeny. 'This is *our* area of jurisdiction.'

'It could be linked to the Norton case,' Olly Simpson pointed out.

'Is that being taken over, too?' grumbled Beeny.

'OK, calm down! Major Pinkney is dealing with it. We've plenty on our hands. Heather has returned to the hospital to insist on seeing and interviewing Norton. That woman *must* be persuaded to talk. We're at a standstill until she does.'

'No, sir, I think we have a strong lead to follow.'

Tom stared at Piercey with suspicion. 'And what's that?'

With surprising constraint, the maverick sergeant outlined what he had done after Jimmy James had identified the car he had seen on the night Norton had been attacked. He produced a sweat towel in an evidence bag.

'The DNA on this can be compared with that on Maria's clothes.'

Still taken aback at Piercey's low-key attitude Tom still put forward some objections. 'That storeman's not a reliable witness. He's changed his mind several times under questioning. The car could have broken down beside the gymnasium and been left to await collection the next day.'

'It could have, but I swear we're on the way to solving the case.' Piercey's normal optimism was starting to return. 'I checked out the owner of the hatchback.'

'And?'

'Sergeant Dennis Maple. It all ties in, sir.'

'Ties in how, and with what?'

'Maple sang the role of Don Jose in the opera. Carmen teases and torments him, flaunts her sexuality, inspires slavish devotion in him. We all saw it as a brilliant portrayal of her role, but what if she was so believable because she wasn't acting? And neither was he?'

'Oh, come on . . .' Tom began.

'I'm serious, sir. Maria was like that. Leading you on, then making you jealous. A lot of us got the treatment. She made it very obvious so that the *real* passion going on between them wasn't noticed. Or it was seen more as successful theatrical coupling, nothing more.'

'Dennis Maple is married with two young children,' put in Connie. 'I interviewed him briefly the following day. He left the party early with his family. His wife was there and agreed they had allowed the children to stay for an hour at the party, then took them home to bed.'

Piercey turned to her. 'Did she say she and Dennis then went to bed?'

'This is all pure speculation,' ruled Tom.

'Until we get a DNA match,' Piercey insisted.

Olly glanced up from his sketching. 'His'll be on her Spanish costume because he'll have touched it during the opera. We won't get anywhere with that.'

For a brief moment Piercey looked defeated, then he bounced back. 'OK, if they took their kids home early after the party what was his hatchback doing outside the gymnasium in the early hours of Sunday?'

'James is an unreliable witness,' Tom repeated.

'Not over anything connected with tailoring,' countered Piercey. 'We've said his brain only works around that subject. You didn't see him last night. He was excited over that sticker on the windscreen. A one-track mind like his would fasten on something like that and make no errors over what he saw.'

There really was a lot in what Piercey said, thought Tom. He knew Dennis Maple only vaguely, not well enough to dismiss this theory out of hand. While watching the opera he had been more intent on how much longer it would go on, but now Piercey had raised the issue Tom acknowledged that the performance passion between Carmen and Don Jose could have been real.

Max had been silent until now, but offered his opinion. 'If it had been instant, overwhelming attraction at the auditions, Maple could have made her pregnant. He would certainly have a need for it to be terminated. A strong enough need to persuade her with violence.'

'There's one more point,' said Piercey, struggling to control his natural arrogance. 'You asked me to think of any incident which might have inspired someone to set me up by using my Audi to pick Norton up that night, and by planting her mobile in it. I racked my brain for something in my professional capacity and drew a blank, but now we have this info about Dennis Maple I think I know what drove him to implicate me and it points to the strong probability that he fully intended to beat her up that night.'

'Go on,' said Tom.

'It was during the interval on Friday night's performance of *Carmen*. I donned the elaborate picador's costume, then I spotted Maria in the wings looking extremely tense. I went over and tried to reassure her. She just stared at me as if she had no idea who I was. Her behaviour bothered me, so I put my arms round her, told her she was superlative tonight. The best so far.

'Next minute, Maple grabbed me by the shoulders and dragged me backstage. He then launched into a spiel about my morals, my reputation; stuff about no woman being safe when I was around.' Piercey's face flushed with revived anger. 'There was a lot more. He didn't mince words.'

He let out his breath slowly before adding, 'When I could get a word in I saw the chorus was assembling ready for curtain up, and I had to join them. But I couldn't walk away like a dog with his tail between his legs, so I told him I was free to pursue any woman I fancied. "OK, I might love 'em and leave 'em" I added, "but I'm not married and I've never fathered any bastards like some I've come across."'

There was a significant silence from the whole team after that statement.

Eventually, Max said, 'So all we have is the identification of that hatchback by an unreliable witness, and a conversation between a suspect and the man who's presently standing accused of the crime; a conversation nobody else heard. As Olly pointed out, Maple's DNA will be on Norton's Spanish costume anyway. Nothing to incriminate him there. We could possibly lift his prints off Phil's Audi, but it's doubtful if a complete one would be conveniently clear enough for our purposes. Even then it would only prove Maple had been in that vehicle *at some time*, not that he had assaulted a woman in it.'

Piercey fired up swiftly. 'We have Staff Andrews' witness statement in which he says he saw Maria jump in my car, then he watched some kind of violent behaviour taking place in it up by the copse.'

'You should be aware of the problems with that,' Tom put in heavily. 'Staff Andrews didn't see who was at the wheel. Neither did Private James who witnessed your arrival at the

Mess, but only saw the vehicle being backed out and driven off ten minutes later. In his statement he says he assumed you had gone to your room to change from the "fancy dress outfit" then went out again. No help there.'

'We can't ignore this,' Connie protested. 'It makes such sense of what we know. Yes, it's circumstantial but I believe Jimmy James *would* recognize that hatchback, because of the sticker. Phil's right. That man's brain lights up like a beacon over anything connected to his main focus in life.

'Our initial round of interviews centred on everyone involved with the opera. We naturally concentrated on single males who had stayed late at the party and were known to have flirted with Norton throughout. As I said just now, I conducted an interview with Dennis Maple in his quarter. He and his family were packing for a trip to Holland starting early the next morning. His wife was present when he told me they had left the party before midnight because the children were tired. His wife agreed, and the rest of the interview revolved around their observations on Norton's relations with the rest of the cast. There was nothing to suggest he could be implicated. However, I now recall that Christine Maple agreed to his account of what they had done that night after he said, "Isn't that right, darling?".'

'You think he challenged her to lie for him?' asked Max.

'No, not that, but he could have been consolidating his alibi.'

'Which he did,' snapped Piercey.

Connie ignored that. 'It would be interesting to know whether they still share a bedroom. If he's been having an affair with Norton, separate rooms would make it easy for him.'

'Hence how he managed to leave his house again in the early hours to meet his lover.' Tom glanced at Max. 'I think we'd be justified in bringing him in for an explanation of why his vehicle was seen near the Sergeants' Mess ninety minutes after he claimed to have returned home from the theatre.'

Max nodded. 'And Connie should follow up on her earlier interview by visiting Christine Maple when she's at home alone.'

As Tom made to agree his mobile rang and he saw the caller was Heather. News from the hospital!

'Has Norton agreed to talk?' he asked briskly.

'No, sir, I'm afraid she's done another runner.'

'*What?*'

They gave her breakfast, but when they went to collect the tray the bed was empty and some clothes are missing. The rest of her stuff is still in the locker. They made a token search, then the flower seller by the main entrance said she saw a taxi collect a young woman who looked ill and distressed.'

'How long ago?'

'She couldn't be sure, but I'd say it must have been Norton.'

'OK, report back here as soon as.'

Disconnecting, Tom broke the news, adding in his personal frustration, 'She's set on killing herself one way or another, silly bitch!'

'Do we put her details back on the system?' asked Beeny.

'I don't think that's necessary,' Max replied thoughtfully. 'She's left the bulk of her things at the hospital where she knows they'll be safely stored until she needs them. When Connie and I visited her the only words she uttered were *I want to come back*. I promised to arrange her transfer but I was thwarted in that by her doctors. I reckon she's taken the plunge and is on her way to the base.'

Almost as he finished speaking his own mobile rang. He listened for several moments, then looked at Tom and repeated what he had been told.

'The guard at the main gate has just called the Medical Centre to say Corporal Maria Norton has arrived by taxi in a state of near collapse, and an ambulance is needed.'

Beeny had been sent to bring Dennis Maple in for questioning, and Tom told Piercey to go to the Mess and stay there until contacted. There was unspoken acceptance that Max should go to the Medical Centre where Maria Norton would again be a patient of his future wife. He took Connie with him, so

Olly Simpson was delegated to track down Christine Maple for some delicate questioning.

Max was glad to learn that Duncan MacPherson was at a regional meeting, which meant Clare was in sole charge until her partner returned in the afternoon. She was completely professional, as was Max, as they discussed the young corporal's return.

'I've informed the doctor who was handling her case that she's here under medical supervision, and asked for her details to be sent over,' Clare said after greeting them. Then to Max, 'I want to make it clear that there's no question of a Redcap sitting outside the ward. My patient is in a delicate physical state and mentally distressed. She has just terminated a pregnancy. Whatever the circumstances surrounding that, it's a traumatic event in a woman's life and I won't have her treated as a criminal.'

Max smiled. 'We're SIB not the KGB. She's returned of her own free will, so there's no likelihood of her going AWOL, and I believe there's no possibility of another assault on her, as we previously feared. Has she given you a reason for her actions?'

Clare shook her head. 'I doubt you'll get much from her. She asked to make a phone call, but I told her she must wait until you've had a chance to talk to her. She clammed up then.'

'How long can we stay?' asked Connie.

'For as long as you can stand her silence. I'm sure I don't need to tell you you mustn't threaten her in any way.'

Connie took that badly. 'Ma'am, I'm a woman, not a bully. I have some notion of what she's been through over the past two weeks.'

'Of course,' agreed Clare in softer tones. 'It's just that she seems to me to be a victim several times over. In my profession I view things differently.'

She walked from her consulting room along the corridor to the ward at the end of it, opened the door, and led them to where the patient lay. Max thought she looked worse than ever, with red-rimmed eyes and chalk white skin between the lingering bruises.

'Go away!' she said in a voice husky from weeping. 'You said you'd get me back here, and you lied.'

Clare answered that. 'I explained to you that Doctor Breck refused to allow you to leave. Captain Rydal tried his best to have you transferred. I suggest you now cooperate with him so that everything can be straightened out and you can begin to recover. It's time you did.'

'Let me make that phone call first. *Please.*'

Clare began to withdraw. 'After you've talked to Captain Rydal and Sergeant Bush. That's a promise, Maria.'

Max remained standing, allowing Connie to take a less official pose on the bedside chair. 'Are you anxious to call your parents?' he asked quietly.

Maria made a slight negative gesture with her head on the pillows.

'Who, then?'

She turned her face to the wall.

'To the father of the baby?' It was said gently, but it surprised Max who had not expected Connie to plunge straight in with something so direct. 'You must want to talk to him very badly about how you feel now you've done what he wished.'

Silence.

'I can't believe the hospital staff prevented you from making that call. They're usually very helpful.'

Silence.

'Was it him you tried to call from the Poppin Eaterie?'

That brought a response. 'How d'you know about that?'

Connie smiled. 'It's part of our job to find people. You were still suffering from the beating you had and we wanted to help you.' Connie waited several moments before repeating the question, then added, 'The café staff saw you make three calls without apparent success. Did he refuse to answer?'

'He wouldn't do that,' she said vehemently.

'Had you arranged to meet him at the Imperial Hotel?'

'I sent a text telling him I'd be there so we could talk again.' Her dark eyes stared at Connie, ignoring the man standing well back from the bed. They were full of desperation. 'He must've been delayed. He wouldn't have . . .' The protest died away.

'But he did, didn't he?' reasoned Connie very gently. 'He failed to come when you most needed him.' She let that sink in for several moments, then probed further. 'And he won't take any calls from you. Why d'you think he's behaving that way, Maria?'

The patient's eyes were growing glassy with tears. It was clear she was near the end of her tether and starting to respond to Connie's sympathetic approach.

'He doesn't know I've done it, because he won't speak to me. I need to tell him. Show him that everything will be back to how it was.'

'I could take a message. You could write him a note, and . . .'

'I did that at the hospital. They couldn't have posted it. I asked a nurse to send an email, but she obviously didn't. He would have come there if she had.'

Once more Max admired Connie's ability to coax people to reveal what they were reluctant to admit. Norton was certain soon to identify her lover, if only by inference.

'Perhaps he was unable to. You know how orders come out of the blue sometimes. Attend a two-week course. Replace someone who's dropped out of an exercise. That kind of thing. Is he liable to get sudden transit orders?'

'Not any more. He was wounded in Afghanistan three years ago, so he's Admin now. He's not happy about it, but he couldn't have been in *Carmen* unless, could he? And we wouldn't have found each other. I *have* to speak to him, tell him it's all right again. I *have* to.'

'Yes, I see that. I'll try to help. Which regiment is he with?'

'The West Wilts. Can you contact him? Get someone to tell him to call me urgently? You can *make* them, can't you? You're police.'

'It doesn't work that way, Maria. I can certainly go and talk to him. Take a note from you, if you like.'

Max's admiration of Connie's professionalism increased further. She had not betrayed to the distressed girl that she had just given out an important piece of information, and was continuing her 'water on a stone' technique which was slowly succeeding. He slipped unobtrusively from the room to text Tom, who was probably interviewing Sergeant Dennis Maple of the West Wiltshire Regiment. Had he been wounded in Afghanistan three years ago?

When he re-entered the ward he saw Maria Norton sobbing against Connie's shoulder while disconnected phrases tumbled from her hoarse throat. Connie signalled with her eyebrows that he should stay in the background, which he was happy to do.

'I was *thrilled*. The baby was a part of him I'd have forever. *Forever*. I thought he'd just love that. He adored me. *Worshipped* me. He'd do anything I told him to do. *Anything*. I was his whole life. Nothing else mattered. He told me that over and over again,' the girl in the hospital bed cried brokenly.

'But it mattered to him that he'd made you pregnant?' murmured Connie, still sending optical signals to Max.

'He was angry when I first told him, but I knew he'd be *thrilled* when we could really talk about our future together. With our baby.'

'But he was still angry when you met him after the last night party?'

Maria pulled away to look at Connie with the pain of incomprehension. She seemed unaware of another presence in the room. 'He was so different,' she whispered. 'The way he behaved. The way he spoke to me. *Shouted*. He'd always been so loving, so anxious to please me. Always afraid I'd not let him do the things he wanted when we met. I'd tease him. He loved it when I did that.' She gripped Connie's hands very tightly with her own that were shaking. 'How could he suddenly be so different?' she begged.

'Did he want you to have an abortion, Maria? Is that what he demanded when you met up after the party?'

There was a long pause before the answer came, and the girl sagged back against the pillows with exhaustion. 'I tried so hard to make him understand how wonderful it was, but he was furious. He said it could be anyone's child. He'd seen me throwing myself at all the men night after night, just to make him jealous. He said . . . he said it was over. Told me to find another bloody fool. Someone like Phil Piercey, who deserved to be lumped with an anonymous bastard.'

ELEVEN

Dennis Maple was angry, unable to control his words and actions. He swore loudly and looked set to defy Beeny's instruction to accompany him to 26 Section Headquarters.

'What flaming for? Some bugger been speaking out of turn?' he demanded, his square face reddening. 'You can't just come in here and tell me I'm under arrest. What right . . .'

'You're not under arrest, Sergeant Maple,' Beeny told him calmly. 'We need to clarify some points in your statement, and we need to do it *now*.'

'Statement? What statement? I've made no bloody statement.'

'I'm here to accompany you to Headquarters, not to argue with you, and I'm getting impatient.'

'So am I, Sonny Jim,' Maple sneered. 'Get your act together and find the right guy who *made a statement*. The *right* guy.'

Derek Beeny took some handcuffs from his pocket and made ready to apply them and, after a swift glance at his interested colleagues, Maple said testily, 'OK, OK, play your little game if it amuses you.' Picking his beret from the hook he pulled it on. 'I'll sort this out with someone more intelligent.'

Having to wait in an interview room while Beeny relayed to Tom the aggressive attitude Maple was in did not improve his mood, so the irate NCO got his protest in the moment the two detectives entered.

'This is bloody insulting! What right have you to treat me like a felon? Give me chapter and verse.'

Tom ignored that and took his time to sit and arrange a file with precise neatness on the table between them. While Maple silently but visibly fumed, Tom went through the formalities before opening the file and reading out the first part of Connie's report.

'*When asked what time he left the party following the final performance of the opera, Sergeant Maple said it was a short while before midnight because his children were tired. His wife, Christine, supported that statement.*' Tom glanced up and felt no surprise on seeing the concern on the man's face. 'Is that correct?'

'What?' Maple now looked dazed. 'What the hell is this all about?'

'Do you stand by that estimate of when you returned to your house after attending the stage party?'

'That woman came on Sunday afternoon when we were packing to go off for a week's break, and asked our opinion of that melodramatic tart Norton,' Maple replied belligerently. 'That's all it was. We weren't *making a statement*, for Christ's sake. It was an *opinion*. What right had she to write it down and file it?'

'Do you own a bronze hatchback with this registration number?' Beeny asked, showing him a computer printout.

Maple's tone subtly changed. 'It says there that I do.'

'So can you explain why a witness saw it parked outside the gymnasium an hour and a half after you claim you drove your family home on that Saturday night?'

'*What*? Who saw it? He made a mistake. Couldn't have seen it there.'

Both Tom and Beeny remained silent, keeping eye contact, as long moments passed and Maple grew restless.

'What's that bitch been saying?' he demanded suddenly.

Still the detective duo maintained their silent scrutiny.

'Someone must have taken the bloody vehicle from outside the house. Yes, of course they did. Kids. Teens. Joyriding around the base in it for fun. Embryo thugs!'

Tom tapped a finger against the report before him. 'Sergeant Bush states here that you and your wife were preparing to drive to Holland when she visited you on Sunday afternoon, so your vehicle was back by then?'

'Yes.'

'Unusually considerate embryo thugs! I've never known joyriders to return a vehicle they've stolen and driven the guts out of. They either wreck it in a smash-up, or trash it before torching the carcase.'

At that point Tom's mobile buzzed to indicate a text coming in. When he read Max's message the inquisition really began.

It took them all day trying to wrest a confession from Dennis Maple, but he was a tough nut to crack. Shortly before sixteen hundred Max received a call from Clare who said Maria Norton was asking for Connie Bush to visit her because she had something important to tell her. Within an hour the accusation of ABH against Phil Piercey had been withdrawn and transferred to Dennis Maple, who instantly denied it. However, by then the team had gathered evidence from Christine Maple, who had known her husband was having an affair with his acting partner so they had been sleeping apart for around two months.

She told Heather, who had teamed up with Olly Simpson, 'Dennis mooned around like a pet poodle waiting for a pat from her. He'd even sit up and beg for it, I shouldn't wonder. He lived in a make-believe world, seeing that woman as a temptress he strove to satisfy. Ugh, it was sickening to see him and her living a fantasy before an audience night after night. The week in Holland was meant to iron things out between us, but it failed and he's been in a foul mood since we got back.'

In some distress she admitted that her husband had a violent temper, but added, 'If he really did beat her up he was still acting his part as the jealous lover in the opera. He's never lifted a finger against me. Or the children. He simply grew obsessed with Carmen.'

Nobody pointed out to her that the opera has Don Jose killing the woman he is obsessed with, not making her pregnant.

After eating the meal Nora had kept hot for him, Tom settled beside her on the sofa to finish the contents of the bottle of wine he had opened on arriving halfway through the evening feeling in need of alcoholic stimulant. They had chatted lightly while he ate, one topic being that Clare had asked Nora to make her dress for the wedding.

'Not a huge billowing affair more suited to a panto fairy queen, I trust,' he had said, munching rhubarb crumble.

Nora had shaken her head. 'I gather she wore something like that when she married her titled husband, because it took place in a cathedral with five hundred guests and an escort of Guards officers in full fig. His family chose the dress and footed the bill.'

'Hmm, the Clare we know doesn't seem the type to be dominated by prospective in-laws.'

'No, but she was very young. I guess she and her parents could have been overwhelmed by the aristocracy and all the swagger of uniforms, coronets and earls in a cathedral. His mother was a real force to be reckoned with, Clare told me.'

'Did they have a twenty-one gun salute?'

Nora made a face at him. 'Now you're being silly. She wants a simple classic long gown in deep cream silk . . . and you're not to tell Max.'

'We men don't waffle on about such trifling things,' he had told her airily.

'No, you *waffle on* about footballers' antics in their hotel rooms, and the new strip club that's opened in town.'

Once they relaxed on the sofa, Strudel in her favourite spot against Nora's slippers, Tom returned to the subject of romance, and *Carmen*.

'Their kinky relationshp went unnoticed publicly because they were acting it out in the opera. In the role of Don Jose he had to be besotted with Carmen, and insanely jealous of any other man she flirted with. She played the role too well, and he really grew besotted with her. In turn, she found she got her kicks from teasing and tormenting him.' He gave a dry laugh. 'In a brothel he'd have to pay to be dominated and taunted, but he got it free from her.'

'Until stark reality hit him,' murmured Nora. 'Men forget to add possible pregnancy in the equation.'

'Oh, birth control wasn't part of the fantasy they were living, love. Remember my telling you the Bandmaster sounded almost orgasmic in describing how realistically Norton played the role?'

'Mmm, and you worried about your virility because you preferred feeling Christopher kick my stomach to watching her.'

'I still prefer feeling your stomach. I can't see what all the fuss is about. She was dressed in revealing clothes and flaunted herself as she sang, but it didn't make me long to have her whip me.'

She chuckled. 'You haven't that much imagination, that's why. You're a standard manly man.' She kissed his ear. 'And I'm glad you are. I'll soon have a fourth child to look after, to say nothing of a mischievous puppy. I don't have time to whip you whenever you fancy a dose.'

He had another sip of his wine, still mulling over the fact that a sticker advertising car dealers with the same name as an upmarket gentlemen's outfitters should have led to that day's revelations. Maple was still denying culpability, but evidence was mounting against him and they would get him eventually. So, with Easter fast approaching maybe 26 Section would have a quiet period once this case was sewn up.

Yet Tom was sure Max was still after a wild goose.

Max and Clare ate at their favourite inn beside the river to celebrate the breakthrough in the *Carmen* case, as it had been known. Clare asked what the consequences for her patient would be.

'She's been through a lot, Max.'

'As have a number of soldiers, but it doesn't make them immune to military law.'

She sighed. 'There speaks the policeman.'

'OK, speaking as a simple male I think she's allowed her conflicting talents for soldiering and singing to make a mess of her life. Certainly of her career in the Army.' He put the cutlery on his plate, leaned back against the *volk*-patterned, cushioned backrest and took up his wine glass. 'She returned from being AWOL of her own accord, and she voluntarily confessed to making a false accusation against Piercey. Obstructing the course of justice. But, in view of the fact that you would probably hold that her mind was so disturbed she wasn't in control of what she said and did, nothing would be gained by pursuing an action against her.

'Tom and I conferred with Keith Pinkney, who had a chat with the Garrison Commander, and the consensus is that the security vetting that allowed her to deal with sensitive or classified signals would have to be withdrawn, and a posting to a backwater job would follow a period of sick leave.' He gave a wry smile. 'She'll be lucky to get away with just that.'

'I suppose so. Maybe she'll leave the Army and concentrate on a singing career.'

He nodded. 'Might be the better option, so long as she avoids *Carmen*.'

'I wish I'd seen her performance. Must have been powerful to have so many men lusting after her. How does Phil feel about her now? Isn't he keen for some kind of redress?'

The waiter came to remove their plates and take their order for dessert. When he moved off, Max said, 'That lecherous lad is still licking his wounds.' He chuckled. 'Being used that way by a woman is not a good experience for someone who regards himself as irresistible to the fair sex. He's eager to let the whole humiliating episode be forgotten. He might have learned a lesson from it, but I reckon he'll bounce back before too long. He's actually a more effective detective that way.'

Two plates containing apricot tart and whipped cream were put before them, and Max ordered coffee to follow. They then spoke about the medical board Max had been summoned to attend on the following Thursday.

Clare said hesitantly, 'Duncan and I agree that he should give you the general check-up they'll require in advance.' As

Max made to speak, she added, 'In view of our changed relationship it's better for an impartial doctor to submit it.'

He gave her an intimate smile. 'You feel they wouldn't approve of your method of proving my full fitness?'

Returning the optical intimacy, she said, 'Mmm, it would be regarded as "alternative medicine", no doubt. Speaking of which, your place or mine tonight?'

'Oh, yours. It's far more cosy.' He frowned. 'We'll have to think about looking for another place. We can't go on living in two separate apartments much longer.'

'No.'

The waiter brought their coffee and withdrew. 'Max,' Clare said quietly, 'I've been thinking over our plan to have a child as soon as possible, and reached a decision.'

His heart sank. She was going to change her mind about having a family. 'I thought you were happy about the idea.'

'I am, darling. Very happy. But when I produce Rydal junior I want to be an old-fashioned mother who stays at home with her baby. I also want to be with you wherever you're serving, so I'll leave the Army at the appropriate time. I can be a civilian doctor anywhere, but you can only be a military detective wherever you're sent.'

Relief and delight mingled, and he gripped her hand across the table. 'Why did it take me so long to see the light where you're concerned? Let's go home and celebrate the fact that I now have.'

Despite their romantic mood, before Max crossed the large shared room to Clare's bedroom he checked Dennis Maple's service record on his laptop. It confirmed what he suspected and completed what had been a very good day.

First thing next morning Max drove to the base and headed for 5 Signals and Lieutenant Su Carfax. On entering her office he was again struck by her exotic beauty, but he was too focussed on chasing a goose to be affected by it now.

She glanced up, then left her seat to walk around the desk to stand before him. 'Thank you for informing us that Norton had voluntarily returned, but I must protest at being refused access to her until the evening. Sergeant Bush was very officious.'

Max nodded. 'According to military law Corporal Norton has committed several quite serious crimes for which she could be charged and punished. While not actually under arrest she is helping with our inquiries into who viciously attacked and abandoned her without the means of summoning help. Sergeant Bush was slowly getting to the truth. Any interruptions at that stage could have halted the confidences Norton was offering.'

Knowing he wanted something from this woman Max softened his tone, and repeated what Clare had said to him yesterday. 'Your corporal has had a difficult time. She's hurting, both physically and emotionally. Our inquiries have given us the impression that she feels very alone. To compensate she seeks attention by trading on her sexual attraction to have men vying with each other. This gives her a satisfying sense of power, but it breeds resentment in other women so that she has no real friends. In her weakened and desperate state she sees Connie Bush as someone who will understand and who she can trust.

'My sergeant is very good at empathizing and encouraging scared people to face up to the truth. So we now have the real identity of her attacker, and an innocent man has been cleared of blame.' He gave a faint smile. 'These kind of interviews need clever, gentle handling, so I'm sure you can appreciate why breaking the continuity for anything other than the most vital reason can be counter-productive.'

The young officer appeared to be mollified and asked if Norton would have to face a court of inquiry. Knowing that to be unlikely, Max merely said nothing had yet been decided because she was still too unwell to take things further. Then he approached what he had gone to discover.

'There was another violent assault two days ago which we thought might be linked to this case, but Norton's new evidence dismisses that theory, so we now have to follow a different line,' he said, hoping she was not aware that the victim had been whisked away before he could be questioned.

'In pursuit of this new inquiry I have to ask you if the classified signal Maria Norton authenticated at noon on the day she was assaulted concerned Captain Rory Smythe.'

Any hint of rapport between them vanished instantly; the expression in her dark eyes hardening. 'Don't you understand the meaning of *classified*, Captain Rydal?'

'This is a police investigation, Lieutenant Carfax. We need all the facts,' he retaliated firmly. 'I'm not asking for the content of the signal, merely if it concerned that particular officer.'

It was useless. She held the aces. 'The need-to-know list didn't bear your name or that of 26 Section.' She returned to her chair behind the desk. 'I'm very busy. Like SIB, we in Signals won't have our work interrupted by anything other than the most vital reasons.'

Max had not expected an answer, and privately commended her refusal to give it, but he was an experienced interrogator and had recognized her fleeting facial signs that told him he had scored. Spurred on by this evidence he drove to Headquarters where Tom and Beeny were preparing to interview Dennis Maple once more. After a brief word with them, he went to his office after collecting a mug of coffee and a sultana and walnut muffin.

He began by accessing the details of the inquest on the death of Private Glenn Fortuna, killed by enemy action in Afghanistan twenty-eight months ago. After studying that very thoughtfully, he again checked Dennis Maple's service record. The coffee grew cold in the mug and the muffin remained uneaten as he matched a series of dates and stared at them with deep concentration. Half an hour later he reached for the red telephone on his desk.

The husky voice which once used to make his pulse race told him he had reached Captain Livya Cordwell. Now all he said was, 'It's Max Rydal. I need to speak to the Brigadier.' Why was it so difficult to say *my father*? 'On his secure line.'

There was a hung moment before she said in her official manner, 'His visitor has just left. Please hold while I advise him of your request.'

Several clicks and they were connected. 'Hallo, Max,' said Andrew with no hint of surprise that his son should be calling him on the scrambler for the very first time. 'A problem?'

'Good morning, sir. Not a problem, I'd just like to run something past you.'

'Go ahead,' came the calm response.

'A school leaver with just six months' service loses contact with the body of a night patrol in Afghanistan and is shot. The corporal leading the patrol goes out to recover the lad and finds him dead, the enemy having apparently silently departed. The Casevac helo arriving to pick him up comes under fire from rocket grenades. A crew member and the corporal are wounded and flown to a field hospital for treatment, thence to the UK.

'Three weeks later the commander of the dead lad's company takes up an appointment as an Aide de Camp. The corporal recovers and resumes service with a different battalion, earning promotion to sergeant. Are you with me so far, sir?'

Just a clipped affirmative, nothing more.

'Twenty-eight months later a conference is held on the military establishment where this sergeant is serving as a non-combatant due to his injuries, and he sees the former company commander who is now an ADC to a general. Late that night the ADC is discovered by the roadside having been viciously attacked. He claims to have no memory of what happened, and he's taken with surprising suddenness to an unknown medical destination.'

'That's a very interesting scenario,' said Andrew, with a suggestion of warmth in his rich voice.

'That's what I thought, sir, and I found it even more interesting when I checked the details of the young lad's fatal injuries. Face and half his skull blown away. Now, when men go out on night patrol in a war zone they blacken that part of their face which isn't protected by their headgear to avoid being an easy target, so the enemy must have been an impossibly brilliant marksman to hit the lad right between the eyes on a moonless night and inflict the kind of injuries more usually sustained when a rifle is placed in the mouth and fired.'

Several moments passed before Andrew said, still in friendly manner, 'This is something you've dreamed up as a poser on an exam paper for police cadets, I take it. They are asked: "a" was the enemy an impossibly brilliant marksman, or "b" . . . ?'

'Was the lad driven to commit suicide by sadistic bullying or homosexual attentions by his company commander who then prudently transferred to a plum job where he was privy to classified, even secret information? And did evidence at a later date confirm that "b" was the correct answer, and was a classified signal to that effect sent to the military establishment where said ADC was hearing details of future combat planning, warning that he should be removed forthwith?

'And "c",' added Max, well into his stride, 'did that man who had crawled out on that dark night and seen the lad's injuries, maybe heard a few dying words, decide to administer rough justice before his victim could be spirited away without anyone being aware of his destination?'

An even longer pause this time before his father spoke. 'It's certainly a most intriguing exercise to ponder over, but I wouldn't use it, Max.'

'Is that by way of a warning, sir?' he challenged.

'No–o, I wouldn't go so far as that. I just feel it's too complicated for trainee policemen. It takes someone with your doggedness and detective skills to unravel such complexities which, you know, have a habit of being dealt with in the time-honoured manner.' Leaving time for that to sink in, he said with real warmth, 'Thank you for running it past me. I found it very enlightening. I'm deeply impressed. The Medical Board is sure to find you in tip top shape.'

Once she began to confide in Connie Bush, Maria Norton had talked non-stop about how she felt she had screwed up her life and she was then persuaded to accept that the love affair had been no more than a fantasy between Carmen and Don Jose.

When the team met at the end of the working day, Connie gave the details of the emotional interview. 'Norton denies being part of a plot to incriminate Phil, and I believe her. She said she stayed late at the party waiting for Maple to phone that he was ready to meet her. A call came in but it was from Staff Andrews, who tried to arrange a meeting. Phil interrupted that call and she told Staff she would call back in ten, which she didn't as he said in his statement.'

Giving Piercey a significant glance, she continued. 'Unprepared for your apparent belief that she would make a night of it with you, she used melodramatic means to drive you away. While she was putting on that performance for the benefit of a group still lingering in the auditorium she missed the call from Maple. With you gone, and Bill Jensen agitating about locking the premises, she called Maple's mobile to explain what had happened and telling him you had just left so she was on her way. The reason he gave her for using the Audi was that there were still people moving around the base, it being Saturday-night-Sunday-morning, so anyone spotting them would believe she was with you.'

'And they'd believe *I* made her pregnant,' put in Piercey with disgust. 'Bastard!'

'He drove to the copse and parked up a short way from the main track,' Connie said. 'Maria told me she was so concentrated on how she was going to paint a wonderful picture of them making a new start together with their baby, she was shocked and disbelieving when he immediately demanded that she had an abortion.'

Including the rest of the team now in her gaze, she continued. 'No need for me to elaborate on how the scene played out. It ran along predictable lines. She had broken the news to him before Friday's performance and been taken aback by his lack of delight, but she put that down to misjudged timing. This hostile demand to rid herself of the result of their passion led her to plead, persuade, and generally use the sexual lures of Carmen which had worked so well over the past two months.'

Connie gave a rueful smile. 'I bet it was some performance,

but reality had returned. Dennis Maple had been shocked out of the persona of Don Jose to face an appalling truth which would complete the break-up of his rocky marriage and land him in a situation he had never envisaged. He wanted out. No arguments!

'Maria told me he first maintained there was no proof the child was his, then poured out a tirade of jealousy of other men in the cast she had played up to, particularly a certain SIB sergeant. This initially delighted her because it gave her that sense of sexual power she revelled in, but he then grew insistent that she must terminate the pregnancy, taking her by the shoulders and shaking her to make his point. When she still refused he grew really vicious, grabbing her around the throat and swearing to choke agreement out of her.'

Connie put aside her notebook and appeared rather upset over what she then had to reveal. 'He dragged her from the car and frog-marched her into the copse, then began a frenzied bout of punching and slapping, telling her he wasn't going to have some man's bastard foisted on him. Walking away, leaving her in a heap on the ground, he warned her either to get rid of it or make Phil Piercey face up to the result of his fornicating.'

Leaving a moment for them all, particularly the Cornish sergeant, to absorb that, she said, 'After being beaten and insulted, Norton accused Phil in order to protect Maple and then went AWOL with the expectancy of meeting him in town to take her to where the abortion could be performed. He didn't turn up – he'd gone to Holland so she booked a room in a seedy hostel used by students. On the wall of the women's toilet was a notice giving the phone number of someone who could "solve the problem many single women face" swiftly and privately.'

She pursed her mouth with disgust. 'I've already contacted the *Polizei* on that, but you can bet the phone number is changed almost daily.' After a heavy sigh she concluded her report. 'Even after suffering that dangerous procedure Norton still wanted to continue a relationship with Maple; still believed all would be sweetness and light once she had done what he drove her to. *Unbelievable!*'

Tom got to his feet and nodded at her. 'You've done well to turn her around and get a signed statement from her. I'm afraid we're having no success with Maple who's denying any involvement in the assault. On the subject of her pregnancy he's sticking to the line that she slept around so anyone could be the father, particularly the SIB sergeant who made his obsession with her so very obvious.' This last was addressed directly at Piercey with no attempt to mask his satisfaction at rubbing-in the fact.

'Jimmy James's sight of that car near the Sergeants' Mess when Maple swears it was outside his house is all we have. In other words, nothing with which to make a case against him. Norton's change of tack wouldn't stand up against Maple's defence. All it does is to allow us legally to remove the charge of ABH against an innocent man. We've had to release Maple for now, but we'll keep at him. He might eventually slip up, or a late witness who's been away on leave or on a course since the end of the opera might come forward with incriminating evidence.' He turned to Max. 'Anything to add, sir?'

'No. I think we all deserve an early night. There's just one thing. I've been given a date next week for my Medical Board, so be prepared for a return to normal the following week,' he announced with a smile.

Olly Simpson murmured, 'We'll advise all wild geese to stay well clear.'

They all laughed and gathered their belongings ready to depart. Tom did the same, but was asked by Max to have a few words in his office. Walking there beside Max, he said, 'You'll have no trouble with the board medics. You'll pass with ease.' He made a wry face. 'I'm sorry I can't hand over a successful outcome to the Norton case. It's been something of a stinker, as you know.'

'Connie's at least got Phil off the hook.'

'Mmm, I wish I could believe it might lead him to take things more seriously and conform.'

'Oh, come on, Tom, he gets results. It's useful to have someone who's a bit of a maverick in a team like ours.' He closed the office door behind them. 'After this we might have a period of more conventional behaviour, but he'll bounce back. The experience might limit his sexual exploits, however.'

'Don't bank on it.' He glanced at the clock. 'What did you want to talk about?'

'Dennis Maple.'

Tom was irritated. Hadn't he just demonstrated that they had no evidence on which to charge him? 'What about him?'

'This is strictly between us, Tom. It's not to become common knowledge. Understood?'

Tom nodded, puzzled. 'Of course.'

He was then told a complex tale concerning a crime that had taken place just over two years ago, but which had had violent repercussions on this base three days ago. While he was still assimilating all the details, Max added a clincher.

'If we can't nail Maple for his attack on Norton he'll go down for the one on Rory Smythe.'

'My God, it all adds up,' he breathed. 'The classified signal we thought was linked to what happened to Norton; the sequestration of the ADC.' He frowned at his friend. 'How on earth did you uncover that?'

Max perched on the edge of his desk wearing the usual happy expression when he actually caught one of the wild geese he chased. 'By noting the state of Maple's hands. His knuckles were bruised and there was evidence of split skin here and there. It was too recent to be the result of the assault on Norton – he had also been on leave for a week since that happened – so I considered the outside possibility that he'd also laid into Smythe. During Connie's questioning of Norton we learned that Maple was non-combatant due to wounds sustained in Afghanistan, so I checked his record and found the incident had occurred when Rory Smythe was his company commander. This tied in neatly with a conversation I had with Guy Strand, who hinted that Smythe was suspected of having unhealthy tendencies whilst out there. After a great deal of cross-checking I reached a conclusion which I ran past someone knowledgeable to gauge his reaction.'

'And?'

Max gave a faint smile. 'He found it very interesting but suggested I let the matter drop, adding that such complicated theories were usually resolved *in time-honoured manner.*'

'And we all know what that means,' grunted Tom.

'Yes. It's a pity we'll get no credit for solving two cases of ABH, but justice will be done which is the important thing.' He gripped Tom's shoulder. 'Let's go home congratulating ourselves on being bloody good detectives, even if no one else on the base will be aware of the fact.'

'Or the rest of our team,' he pointed out sourly.

'Ah, Tom, in our privileged job facts tend to leak out from higher echelons which, with our skills in putting two and two together, will surely enlighten our colleagues and give them an element of satisfaction a few months from now.'

Despite Max's upbeat attitude Tom drove home heavy with a sense of failure. The Norton affair had been his major case during the four months he had been in command of 26 Section and he had been unable to produce a result. Connie had basically been responsible for the main breakthrough, and Max had picked up on Maple's bruised knuckles, which he had not. He could not follow the suggestion that he should congratulate himself on being a bloody good detective, dismissing the skill with which he had directed the team throughout.

Nearing his house he told himself even top CID teams were often denied results due to lack of solid evidence in major cases. It was simply the way things panned out. Nothing to do with the aptitude of the investigators.

He turned the vehicle into the short close and saw a car was parked in the driveway of his house. Someone there for the fitting of a wedding gown. Nora had several on the go, along with bridesmaids' dresses ready for Easter weddings. She was always busy at this time of the year.

He parked in the road, headed for the front door, inserted the key and pushed it open. The house was unusually quiet and his three daughters were huddled together on the third step of the stairs. They gazed at him with wide-eyed, scared expressions.

'What's up?' he asked sharply as some unidentifiable fear quickened his pulse.

The answer came from upstairs. The first cry of a new-born baby! 'Dear God,' he breathed and pushed past them to race up to the next floor and the master bedroom. Thrusting open the door, he was greeted by the sight of Nora lying amid the bloody aftermath of having just given birth.

Even as he registered that she was smiling at him, Clare Goodey said, 'Perfect timing, Tom. Go and show your girls their new brother while I make Nora presentable enough to receive all your congratulations. Placing the blanket-wrapped boy in his arms she physically propelled him back through the doorway. 'I'll shout when you can all come up.'

Hardly aware of what he was doing Tom gazed at the red, wrinkled face of his son, murmuring, 'I've waited so long for you, little fella, then you arrive in a great rush before I am ready.'

The girls suddenly clustered round him to gaze at the baby with the wonder of every person who sees a tiny human being just minutes old. Maggie said in a wobbly voice, 'We were frightened, Dad. We came in from school and Mum was lying on the floor grunting and panting.'

'We didn't know what to do,' added Gina, very pale-faced.

'*I* knew what was happening,' Beth announced. 'It was just that it was too soon. Mum had already called Captain Goodey. She arrived about ten minutes after us. I wanted to see Christopher being born, but she wouldn't let me.'

'Mum made an awful lot of noise,' murmured Gina. 'I thought she was dying.'

Nature-loving Beth glared at her. 'Don't be stupid. Everything does that when having babies. You should hear those pigs down at the farm. I think making a big noise helps,' she added calmly. 'Dad, can I hold our brother?'

'Later,' he said softly. 'There'll be plenty of opportunities.

I'll keep him until we go in to Mum. Then I'll give him to her. She'll want to have a proper look at him, don't you think?'

Clare eventually opened the bedroom door and invited them in. Nora held out her arms for her new son and Tom handed her the child whose conception had been totally unplanned, knowing that Christopher was the perfect gift to complete their family. Momentarily overcome by emotion, he turned away to hide the tears that threatened. What did professional laurels matter when a man had all he had been blessed with? Turning back to study the bundle in Nora's arms his mind began to fill with notions of all he and his son would do together in the coming years.

Max was surprised to find Clare's parking bay empty when he arrived home. Her car had not been outside the Medical Centre, so he had assumed she would be there preparing their meal. He entered his own apartment, changed into casual clothes, then wandered across the shared room to enter her kitchen. Studying the contents of the fridge to find those items which could be prepared in the shortest time, he was still making a choice when she came through her front door.

'Hallo! where've you been?' he asked, going to kiss her, then being surprised when she turned a loving greeting into something much more passionate. Holding her away he studied her glowing expression, the blue sparkle in her eyes, the essence of excitement she exuded. 'Where *have* you been?' he repeated, puzzled.

'I've just delivered Christopher Edward Black, slightly premature but lusty enough and perfect in every detail, to a lovely and loving family which is surely now complete in every way.'

Moving to close the fridge door he had left open, she said, 'Forget home cooking. Let's go to our special inn to celebrate his safe arrival.' Turning back to kiss him very thoroughly again, she said softly, 'Then let's come home and set about making one of our own, darling.'

*   *   *

While Max and Clare were 'wetting the baby's head' at the inn beside the river, and the Black family ecstatically welcomed their newest member, Sergeant Dennis Maple was in a military aircraft heading for the UK, flanked by two soldiers wearing the famous red-topped cap.